Whisperings

Whisperings

A Novel by Barbara Elliott Snedecor

Bookcraft

Salt Lake City, Utah

Library of Congress Catalog Card Number: 90-80497

ISBN 0-88494-737-8

2nd Printing, 1990

Printed in the United States of America

For Steven, Peter,
and Elizabeth

. . . And, behold, the Lord passed by, and a great and strong wind rent the mountains, and brake in pieces the rocks before the Lord; but the Lord was not in the wind: and after the wind an earthquake; but the Lord was not in the earthquake:

And after the earthquake a fire; but the Lord was not in the fire: and after the fire a still small voice.

—1 Kings 19:11-12

1

My beginnings were unremarkable.

I was as normal as they come, growing up in southern Orem, an ordinary Mormon, safe and secure in the shadow of the everlasting hills, protected by the loving warmth of my family, nourished by their kindness and care.

And yet, even before I could possibly understand them, I was taught extraordinary concepts — ideas that suggested I was anything but ordinary. I was blessed — chosen — a child of God, sent to earth at this dispensation in time to fulfill a grand and glorious mission. I was a member of the true Church.

The concepts were warming — reassuring — wonderful, and were grasped by my early mind with wonderful ease, with simple childlike zeal. How I loved to consider my pre-existent beginnings.

Life, though, is often filled with unexpected blessings, unsought experiences, random opportunities tinged with raw pain that distill like vapor into our deepest fibers and linger there forever, changing us, maturing us. We cannot often sense from our beginnings where our ending will find us.

I began such a journey into the unknown in mid-adolescence. Doubt and uncertainty began to creep into my mind like the distant, gray mists of rainclouds

*that could be seen down the valley long before they
dampened the streets near my home.*

*Somehow I sensed my storm approach in the form
and figure and speech of Jilligan Mitchell.*

Jilligan moved into our high school during my junior
year. I sensed there was something different about her
from the moment we met.

She was very pretty, and we surely had enough beautiful girls in our high school for me to sense her intrusion
as painful. She had the kind of long, light brown hair
that crinkled down her back in pleasing waves of softness, draping itself over the back of her chair in lengthy
cascades. I wore my hair short, preferring to wash it and
shake it dry into its close curls, wanting only ease and
convenience. Jilligan's hair made me wonder about
such things as practicality and femininity.

We first became acquainted in Mr. Enfield's AP
American History class. I was afraid to know her,
although I don't think I realized it at first. It was this
business of sensing, as I did, that there was something
unfamiliar about her. She wasn't a Mormon, of course.
And her speech had an unmistakably Eastern sound to
it.

Jilligan held her shoulders so straight and high all
the time, her waist was so thin and fine, her eyes so
bright. And when she raised her feminine hand to respond to a question, her answer was always perfect and
right, tinged with that Kennedy accent that intimated
her non-Wasatch Front origins.

Mr. Enfield loved her.

"Katherine," Jilligan said, turning in her chair to
speak to me, her long hair tumbling behind her in a
quiet flurry.

"I need a friend," she said.

Her soft statement filled me with astonishment. This
new and beautiful girl—this stranger from another
world, another time, another planet, this lovely and fragile girl with the even white teeth, the artfully applied
makeup—wished to find a friend? In me? But I was so

2

ordinary. So unsure of so much. Why should she seek me out?

"What did you say?"

It was impossible to believe what I had heard.

"Are you being funny?"

Jilligan shook her head slightly and glanced quickly at the floor. Her hands gripped the back of her chair, her fingers curled under the plastic back of the seat. I knew then that she was not joking.

"I'm sorry," I babbled on. "It's just so weird. You," I paused, struggling, "you . . ." But I could not say what I was thinking. How could I? What sixteen-year-old girl would admit to another how utterly perfect the other seemed, how she represented to me all that was Eastern and unknown and smarter and surer and, I had to admit, more attractively worldly than anything I had known.

Jilligan made a hard, short sound, the kind I later came to recognize as her painful laugh.

"Jilligan! Katherine!" Mr. Enfield called to us. "Is your conversation for common knowledge?"

Mr. Enfield had that unpleasant way about him, the way so many teachers have. He thought the whole world revolved around American history and that all his students should pay him obeisance for his superior knowledge. Our little thoughts were nothing compared to the revolutionary war.

Jilligan turned quickly in her seat, her waist-long hair swishing behind her, swaying even after Mr. Enfield began his monologue.

And I kept wondering, throughout the long, tedious, unremarkable lecture, why Jilligan would say such a thing to me.

Auntie Anna moved across the street from us when I was four. I called her *Auntie* right from the beginning, even though there was no blood relationship between us. Our connection even then was one of mind, and of heart, and of spirit—a connection that grew stronger with the passing years.

Auntie lived in a house just like ours, except hers had only two bedrooms. Ours had five, because my father kept adding on to our little frame house until it seemed to sprawl all over our small lot in burgeoning disarray. Where the house hadn't spilled, my father grew a careful garden — with raised beds and trellises and dark earth producing food for our family. I spent half my childhood there, it seemed, with my hands in the black, moist earth, where all was fecund and sweet.

Auntie visited my father often in his garden, exchanging successes and failures and hopes for their little plots of beloved soil. They both loved dirt under their nails. Unlike my tall and broad father, Auntie was slim and delicate. And she had diabetes, some sort of ailment that wouldn't allow her to eat cake or ice cream or anything sweet. At six, I couldn't imagine a disease more horrible.

And Auntie didn't see well, either. As a matter of fact, she couldn't see out of her left eye at all. She had a habit of turning her head on an angle when she spoke to you, looking at you from her better eye.

Then, sometime during my eighth year, Auntie went completely blind. The fact that she could no longer see was impossible for me to accept, much less understand. She had to give up her job as an English teacher at Provo High after she lost all her sight.

My mother tried to explain to me why Auntie couldn't see anymore, but it was inconceivable, of course, that anyone should simply *stop* seeing.

"Did she do something bad to her eyes?"

Perhaps she had fallen on some scissors, or had sprayed some poisonous cleanser into her eyes. Maybe she had been hit with a baseball or had been punched in her eyes.

"Well," my mother paused, stopping her potato paring and looking towards Auntie's house, "the diabetes has gradually taken away her sight." My mother tried to explain to me something of blood and of sugar and of old age and of complications of diabetes, but it was clear to me that even my mother didn't understand completely the whys of Auntie's blindness.

4

"But why did Heavenly Father have to do that to Auntie?"

I saw Auntie's blindness as having a direct relationship to Heavenly Father, as if He somehow had ordained her not to see. But it was hard to imagine that anyone as good and giving and jolly as Auntie should suddenly deserve to be blind. Why would God pick *her* — my kind, generous Primary teacher who always had a treasure hunt and ice cream blow-out for the kids in her class.

This was *my* year for the blow-out. Now she couldn't see, and she probably wouldn't have the party anymore. It was very unfair.

The sisters in Relief Society seemed to move into Auntie's home during those weeks, helping her to adjust to her blindness and her early retirement. My own mother and father were often going towards or coming back from Auntie's house, too, just "checking," as they called it, to make sure she was all right.

The lights still went on in Auntie's house at night. And things never looked any different inside or out, although Auntie Anna looked very different to me, with her black glasses and her cane.

The first time she came into our Top-pilot class to teach us again, after several months off to "adjust," as Sister Stott, our Primary president, had called it, I was frightened to have her back. Sister Stott had told us not to worry, and I had seen Auntie dozens of times already. I had sat on her couch and savored her candy (she always had some sitting in a bowl on her coffee table as a treat for visitors) while my mom had helped her unpack her weekly groceries. But now — the sound of her cane coming up the hallway, her steps uneven, the sight of her hand lightly brushing the wall and the doorframe as she entered our class — now I felt afraid, overwhelmed by the change in my wonderful teacher.

"Katherine?"

She called out my name as she paused in the doorway.

"Would you help me locate the table and chair?"

What should I do, I thought, panicking, my heart beating fast.

5

"Don't be afraid, dear Katherine. Just take my hand and be my eyes, will you, dear?" There was a little tremor in Auntie's voice.

I stood then, walked over to my teacher and took her hand. She moved my hand to her elbow.

"Just guide me, dear, as you've seen your mother do. I'm really quite good at finding my way, you know."

I got her safely situated in her chair.

"Thank you, dear."

She proceeded to call on my six other classmates, one by one, asking each of them to help her locate some part of the classroom—the window, the light switch, the chalkboard, the garbage can. We all took our turns guiding her around the room, watching her feel the walls, the window, memorizing in her mind, I realized, the simple lines of the classroom that were so obvious to us.

We didn't have a traditional midweek lesson that day. We learned, instead, about how it felt to guide a person who was blind, how her hands felt, her elbows, the way she held her head, the unexpected tremor that filled her voice now and then, the way her laugh was still the same. She held each of us, that day, before we left her classroom, in her warm and ready embrace, and we felt the reassuring lumpiness of her sweater, the pleasant sweet fragrance that still belonged only to Auntie Anna.

And she told us about the Savior that day, about how, if He wanted, the touch of His hand could make her see again.

I knew then, with the pure, simple faith of a child, that Auntie Anna was right. Surely Jesus would heal her eyes. Surely He loved her very much. It was very obvious in that moment.

Krestin was two-and-a-half years older than I. And he was two inches taller. I always thought I would catch up in both areas, but I never did.

In elementary school, we spent lazy afternoons in the spring and summer standing in the park outside Cherry Hill School in the easy give-and-take of our batting practice. Mount Timpanogos looked over us with its green-brown hugeness as my pitches zinged perfectly over the plate. Though I understood theoretically the concept of a good pitch and a good swing, Krestin was always much better than me in practice.

I talked. He listened. I theorized. He practiced and perfected my theories. He got to be pretty darn good.

We'd walk the back way up to Smith's and Grand Central after practice, just west of the University Mall, and he'd buy me a cone at Snelgrove's with his paper route money.

"You're the best darn coach I could ever ask for," he said.

"You've got talent, Kres," I said.

"Do you really think so?"

"Sure I do."

"Sometimes I really want to do something big with my life. Play in the major leagues or something like that." His bright eyes burned with an endearing intensity. "You know what I mean, Kath?"

I didn't know what he meant at all, but I kept silent. How could he think he could do anything important? We were just ordinary kids, him and me. We grew up in Orem, Utah, no less, out in the middle of nowhere.

"Maybe be famous. Do you think we could be famous?"

I couldn't imagine it at all. We would just get married —maybe to each other—have children, and buy one of the houses in our neighborhood that seemed always to be for sale. And we would keep the commandments.

"We can do anything we want to, you know. We've got all the truth, all the answers anyone could want."

Krestin's cone had a hole in the bottom, and the ice cream was running out of it, dripping onto the ground and onto his sneakers. I didn't know how to tell him about it—he was so involved with his being important, and I was just a dull and normal fourth-grader. I knew nothing.

"Kres," I began to tell him. But it was too late.

"Gee whiz, Kath, why didn't you tell me I was making a pig of myself?"

"Sorry," I said, shrugging my shoulders. "You were being famous and all, and I didn't notice it until a few seconds ago, anyway."

"My mother will shoot me." He screwed up his face in a funny grimace and made his voice go shrill.

" 'Your brand new sneakers!' "

He put his hands on his hips, the way only a mother can. He shook a hand in mock exasperation.

" 'I just can't keep up with the messes in this family. Honestly!' "

Krestin came from a large family of C-Cs. Everyone in his family—and there were eight of them—all had first names that started with C. Except Krestin's, of course, although his might as well have started with C. Krestin Carver, Catherine, Camille, Carl, Charles, Carol —and the parents, Connie and Charles, Sr.

Apparently C was important to them, but I thought it was a dumb thing to do to a family.

Krestin hated it when I called him Kres, but I couldn't call him Krestin all the time. It sounded too much like a movie star, or maybe some character from a book. Or, sometimes, even a girl.

Besides, we were friends. Even when boys and girls weren't supposed to be friends anymore, we were still friends. And I guess that's why we became boyfriend and girlfriend as soon as my magical sixteenth year arrived.

What else was there to do?

We were destined to be together, Krestin told me.

There would be comfort and security in our status as boyfriend and girlfriend, I finally decided, as I took the weekend to think about his romantic Friday evening question. While others plotted and planned and flirted and fooled, I would enjoy the tranquility of good old Krestin's pleasant hand to hold.

And I told him so, when he stopped over that Monday evening in September after our family home evening.

"Hello, Krestin," my father said, his right hand extended in greeting, his left hand holding a plate mounded with whipped cream and strawberries and

8

Mom's best shortcake. "How's the BYU freshman doing this evening?"

Krestin shook my father's hand eagerly, grinning in response.

"Don't you think family home evening is really more for fathers, Kres? I mean, what would life be without these super desserts?"

Krestin and my father laughed hard, but I felt something crackling uncomfortably in my female mind.

And later, when Krestin approached me for my response to his unanswered query, I felt a renewed hesitancy fill me as I spoke.

"Yea, Krestin," I said uncertainly, standing in our backyard garden in between the beans and the tomatoes. "I guess it's okay. I mean, I think it will be fine."

"Hey, don't make it sound like such a death sentence. You don't have to go with me. I'm sure I could find somebody else." He said it with a great big smile—I guessed his comment was supposed to be funny—but his smile faded as I felt my own features turn irrepressibly stern.

"Don't get me wrong, Katherine. I don't want to find anyone else. You're the only one for me."

Krestin wanted to kiss me then, I sensed, but I wanted nothing of it. And so we shook hands, instead. He did have a pleasant handshake.

Ffffffffttt!

I heard the sound of air rushing, then ducked instinctively as I knew my father's sprinkler system would suddenly come into action. Krestin knew it, too, and we both sprinted, laughing, down the little garden path and onto the sidewalk.

"Is that your father's idea of a joke?"

"They come on every night at this time," I answered, in between my laughs.

He was a good, old friend, I thought, as I watched him jog down the block towards his home on 1800 South. I really would rather go with him than with anyone else. It wasn't exactly high romance, of course, this decision of ours to go together, but it was okay. It would be nice to tell people I was going with him, especially now that he was at BYU.

It would be okay.

But as Krestin's figure disappeared around the corner at 543 East, I wondered suddenly what Jilligan would think of him.

2

How strangely hindsight serves us!

Looking back, I see so clearly how the pieces came together that year — how Krestin and Jilligan brought confusion and uncertainty to my mind, and how Auntie brought the peace.

How all-knowing, all-seeing are our remembrances! Yet how limited is our vision for the moment in which we live.

Mr. Enfield finished his lecture on the preliminary events leading up to the revolutionary war. I took my notes with less diligence than usual. I kept contemplating the long hair in front of me once again, wondering what it was like to wash so much hair, and how often it had to be done.

I wondered, too, about the peculiar message Jilligan had shared with me the Friday before. Surely it was all some kind of mistake.

Here I had been wondering about this girl for days, this newcomer to Orem, to our high school; this stranger who smacked of someplace different, whose entrance into our school was more an unwelcome invasion than anything else. For Jilligan had made me wonder about what was out there beyond the safe and everlasting hills. Was it any different than what I knew here?

11

I looked over her shoulder at her meticulously neat and elegant handwriting. How would our conversation go today? Should I just ignore what she had said before? Wait for her to pick things up again? I wanted to tell her about Krestin, but what would she think?

I turned my attention back to the class. I thought how absurd it was that some textbook had given Mr. Enfield the right to label certain events as somehow being the causes of the revolutionary war. Did the colonists know that what they were doing was going to cause a war? Weren't they just reacting to things around them? Now I was going to have to memorize all this stuff as if here were the irrefutable reasons why the colonists went to war. Who could say what caused something, anyway?

The bell interrupted my meandering thoughts. I gathered my stuff and wondered for a moment where I was due to go next.

"Jilligan Mitchell!" Mr. Enfield called.

Jilligan was gathering up her books, putting them back in her knapsack in her slow, precise way. I thought perhaps she was delaying the moment when we would confront one another again. But Mr. Enfield's voice removed that possibility.

"Here he goes again," Jilligan said to me under her breath. "I swear that man has some kind of crush on me. Every day he wants to talk to me about something! Isn't that crazy?"

I agreed that it was, and I thought about it as I wandered down the hall to my locker. I had gym next, and I liked to empty out my bookbag beforehand, preferring to squeeze only my clothes into the insufficient locker at the gym.

It did seem strange that Mr. Enfield should speak to Jilligan so often. I had even noticed it myself. It was only the third week of school—the days still warm with the late glowing, lengthy afternoons of summer—so he really couldn't have any serious business to discuss with her. And yet he seemed to call her to his desk after almost every class.

12

"That man!" It was Jilligan's voice, of course, coming up behind me as I stuffed my things into my locker. "He wanted to know what I thought of his lecture. Can you believe that? What does he think I am? Some sort of historian—just because I come from Boston? It's ridiculous."

"You're from Boston?" I said.

"Couldn't you tell? It seems like all I've gotten since we moved here is comments about how strange I sound." She looked me right in the eye. "Do I really sound that funny?"

"Not at all," I replied. And I meant it. "I kind of like the way you sound. It's different."

"Oh, I'm different all right. Couldn't you tell by the stupid comment I made to you on Friday? You must have thought I was some kind of a nut, asking you to be my friend like that. Like we're back in the first grade or something."

I couldn't determine what the tone in Jilligan's voice meant. I had wanted to know more about her, and her invitation to be her friend had seemed more an honor to me than anything else.

I wasn't in dire need of friends, but there was this unaccounted-for interest in Jilligan that I'd had right from the start. Or maybe it was jealousy, although I didn't dare recognize it as such. Whatever it was that had attracted me to her, I had to admit that even with all her beauty she did seem always to be by herself. She did seem to need someone to talk to, despite the high tilt of her head and the fine way she held her shoulders back.

"Why don't you speak up more in class, Katherine?"

"Huh?"

"I mean, you're obviously very bright. Why don't you ever say anything? You should let people know what you're thinking."

"Huh?" I felt my face turning in on itself in an incredulous way. What on earth was she talking about?

And what a tender nerve she had struck in me. How I longed always to say what was on my mind, to speak the thoughts that rampaged through my head in seminary, for instance. But it felt so risky, so full of effort, and I was too nervous to speak. I was afraid of sounding dumb, or —worse yet—of being wrong. Yet so many times my thoughts turned out to be good ones, or my unspoken questions haunted me for weeks without answers, and I hated myself for not speaking my thoughts.

"You really are something," I said.

Was it that obvious that I was an insecure, intimidated wreck? How did she know that about me?

Bluntness—unexpected, unanticipated, inescapable bluntness—was Jilligan's trademark, I learned that day. It was something I would have to deal with in the months to come.

Auntie Anna was working in her front yard when I walked home from the bus stop. She was on her knees, her hands brushing the surface of the soil lightly. Her right hand deftly snatched at the tiny blades of grass that interrupted the black soil of her garden. She was weeding flower beds that already were lovely beyond description, the roses still abundant, the impatiens spreading out in endlessly scattered loveliness, the ground covers interwoven beneath them.

Auntie provided the flowers every Sunday for sacrament service—large, delicate arrangements that she then delivered to someone in the ward who was sick in some way, their beauty given freely to grace a bedside or a table.

"Home early, aren't you, dear?" she called.

I was used to the way she knew the footsteps of most everyone on our block. She was, quite obviously, the one who truly could see, despite her blindness.

"Auntie!"

I wanted to tell her how remarkable she was, how incredible and wonderful I thought her life was, the feelings flooding me, but instead, tongue-tied, I answered, "I guess I am. I just came home on the regular school bus."

"No meetings of the paper or the yearbook?"

"Not today. Just a dull old ordinary day." I paused then, remembering Jilligan. "Except for one thing."

14

"What's that?"

I told her about Jilligan, about our conversation, about the strange interest I'd had in this newcomer, and about the eerie way she'd chosen me for her friend. I had never experienced anything like it, I told Auntie, as if some unexplainable force had placed us together, and I had little chance to back out. We would be friends.

Auntie thought I was being a little dramatic.

"But I really feel that way, Auntie, as if I should be her friend for some reason."

I told her all that I'd learned about Jilligan, most of it gleaned during our conversation by our lockers. I learned how her father was here consulting for a year with some company, and how he'd decided to bring out his wife and daughter and rent a small home in Orem.

"He's home so sporadically, anyway," Jilligan had said with annoyance. "Who really cares whether we're near his business or not? Half the year they're on the verge of divorce, anyway. I wish he'd left us home in Boston for the year."

I told Auntie how I had marvelled at how naturally that large word, *sporadically,* had come out of her mouth. Four-syllable thoughts were often in my head, but rarely could I force them out of my mouth. Somehow, large words seemed to roll off Jilligan's tongue easily, so pleasantly, as if big thoughts were rightfully spoken among high school students.

Auntie laughed at me.

"Of course you can speak what you feel," she said abruptly, as if she were scolding me. "You've got to start doing that, Katherine, or people will never know what you're thinking. You've so much good to give to the world." Softening, she added, "But I do remember feeling the same way as you—all self-conscious and tongue-tied and unsure. A regular mess." We laughed.

"Don't you think it's strange what she said about her father?" I asked Auntie after we stopped chuckling together.

"Not really, Kathy. What's stranger, probably, is the relationship you have with your family. Yours is the exemplary Mormon home, you know, with devoted parents who serve the Lord and love their children. And their children seem to love them. That's not the way it always is."

"But I have trouble talking to my parents sometimes, too."

"I'm sure you do, Kathy. Still, it's hard to imagine wishing you could be away from your father for a whole year. Not all children grow up nurturing roses and vegetables with their father, Katherine."

I guessed not.

I told Auntie that Jilligan's family still owned their old Victorian home in the Back Bay section of Boston, wherever that was. They would return there at the end of her father's assignment—probably next June.

"Wouldn't you love to see Boston, Auntie?" I said.

Auntie laughed at me again—that quiet, compassionate, wonderful laugh.

"I felt so stupid, Auntie. Here she was talking about Victorian houses and Back Bay and some funny-sounding marketplace and Paul Revere's silver and Harvard and Cambridge and Lexington, and all I could think of was what can I show her out here? And what *can* I show her out here?" I asked in exasperation.

Auntie had finished her gradual, steady movement down the garden bed. She stood now, with a hand on her lower back, and struggled to unbend her body from its crouch.

"These bones, Katherine. These old, old bones."

She held out her elbow and I reached to guide her, a natural reflex. We strolled down the sidewalk to the front walkway to her house.

"Actually, Katherine," she said with a chuckle, "I'm the wrong woman to ask about showing someone the sights in Utah, you know."

She turned her head in my direction, the dark glasses covering her useless eyes, and my heart felt the sudden stab of my foolishness.

It was often like that. The metaphors of sight were so much a part of our language. They stung me sharply when I spoke them to Auntie.

16

"Oh, Auntie! I'm so sorry!"

"Why must you apologize every time you say something like that? For goodness' sake, I ought to know about the failures of language." We slowed at the front steps. She gripped the railing.

"I had sixty-three years of wonderful sight, and I'm not really complaining. But just make sure you don't complain about the things you can't see in Utah. You live in the middle of some of the most beautiful scenery in the world, and yet a few days ago you were belly-mouthing about what your sister was seeing and doing in Logan. Why is it that you always want to be somewhere else?"

Auntie opened her screen door.

"I understand your restlessness," she said, in parting, as the door closed between us, her features shadowed by the mesh. "It's okay to be restless. That's part of growing up."

Then even my restlessness was ordinary, I thought bitterly as I crossed the street.

I looked at my home with critical eyes as I faced it across the lawn. Would Jilligan still want to know me if she saw where I lived?

What would she think of my traditional home, my devoted mother, my father who worked two jobs to support us, my brother on a mission, my sister married, my two little brothers always ready for a tussle? We were so normal.

And what did it matter, anyway, whether Jilligan liked me for me or not? She'd be gone in a year. A short-term investment of self was all that was required. I would keep our friendship low-key and unimportant.

I had idly thought that perhaps Jilligan could fill the gaping female wound in my heart that had been there since my sister had married and left for Logan with my brother-in-law. But there was clearly no chance for that. Jilligan and I were too different. This was a friendship that would fade quickly, with no lasting effect.

I heard the sound of Kres's car pulling up in front of our house. He had a '72 VW "Bug" that he'd modified

17

into one of those Baja types. He had a large, silver chrome muffler on the back, the same size as the one that had dangled from the bottom of my father's station wagon. It was a cute car, although the silver muffler did little to quiet the roar of the exposed and modified engine.

I heard the doorbell ring, followed by the sound of my mother's voice as she greeted him. My little brothers came running, tackling him with affection.

Everyone loved Krestin. He filled in nicely for the big brother who was off in Japan.

"Mrs. Gardner, you have the sweetest-smelling home in all of Orem, I'm sure."

"I don't know about that, Krestin," my mother responded with a smile in her voice. "I'm sure there's at least a half-dozen mothers on this block alone with wonderful aromas pouring out of their kitchens this afternoon. That's how we show off our perfect motherhood." My mother laughed at her joke.

"Well, let's go see, then," Kres responded. "Billy, you start on that side of the block, and Jim, you start over here. We'll all get back together in ten minutes and tally up the smells."

Jim and Bill were already tumbling out of the front door, eager to complete their assignment in record speed. Dropping in on the neighbors was what they loved to do best, anyway.

Mom ran out of the front door after them.

"He's only kidding, you two! Get back here!" There was a pause, followed by a more urgent sound to my mother's voice, and a strong, "Now!"

By now I had come out of my room, gladly abandoning the homework I had been attempting to finish before dinner.

"Hello, my sweetheart!" Krestin's face, like his greeting, was full of innocent exuberance. He bowed graciously.

"How's my lovely lady today?"

Was I really his sweetheart? I didn't feel any different than before.

"I'm afraid I've started another ruckus over here."

"As usual. You do have a real talent for rousing up my little brothers, Krestin. Of course, they're pretty easy to rile up."

Krestin was grinning widely, looking out of the front screen door at the sight of my mother holding on to the hair on each of my little brothers' heads.

"Krestin," she said, with exasperation edging her voice, "please think before you come up with another one of your diabolical plans. Or at least consult me before you suggest them to these two."

"Sure, Mrs. G." Krestin seemed almost genuinely repentant. Then he added quickly, "You're not really upset, are you?"

"No, not really." My mother laughed, and it was good to see her laugh. Dad's long hours and their "concern over finances," as she and my father called it, had sobered her up lately, I felt, pushing her into a kind of mournful, determined mood.

"I'll leave you two alone," she said. "Or as alone as you can manage to get in this house!"

"We'll just sit on the front steps for a while, Mrs. G., and watch the kids run wild through the neighborhood."

But we didn't end up on the front steps at all. We let Bill and Jim talk us into walking with them to the playground—and we were easily persuaded. We naturally gravitated to that spot, anyway, on lazy fall afternoons.

Krestin reached for my hand as we walked down the blocks, trailing far behind my little brothers.

"You know, Katherine, I feel so completely happy with these autumn days, don't you? I just love them so much. We should climb Timp together, don't you think, this fall? Maybe in a few weeks, when the aspens are really quaking. Or at least climb up to the cave before it closes. Some Saturday? Like we used to do."

Krestin went on in his likable way, pushing my little brothers on the swings, scrambling up to the top of the hill with them, then running down it with hands flying high in the air. I sat and watched it all, a part of me celebrating with them, loving the three of them so very much.

But later that same night, alone at my desk under the fluorescent glow of my lamp, my mother already in bed, the house asleep, I wrote these words in my journal.

"Krestin celebrates the simplicities of life like no one else I've ever known. Watching him run down the hill in the playground with my brothers was like receiving a revelation, I think. Though I sat quietly at the base of the hill, in the pleasant relief of a shading tree, I felt in the quiet part of me a complete oneness with life and their living of it.

"How grand it is to be alive, to think and feel and taste and touch. Yet how sad it is to feel something changing, some intangible something rearranging itself within me, wanting more, somehow, than just the simplicity of running down hills with arms overhead, outstretched.

"But what is it that fills me now, even with its absence? Why am I so restless, so hungry to know — completely and assuredly — what makes me worthwhile, what makes my life worthwhile? Is it the idea of being a child of God, with some vested right in His kingdom? Is that really true? And what am I going to do with this life of mine? I want to know so much. Do so much. Yet I can't even open my mouth to speak half the time. And now I've got Jilligan to reckon with.

"Oh! where will life take me? I am one strange kid, I guess. How am I going to figure it all out?"

To the side of my desk, above my small bookcase, hung my favorite picture of the Savior — the one where He is descending amidst the trumpeting angels.

"I Will See You Again," the words beneath the painting said.

Would we *really* see Him again?

3

I feel it now—an airless sense of wonder diffusing time and space and thought—when the strength of my faith overwhelms me, myself abounding with the quiet truths of salvation, a treasured moment of light and knowledge.

That afternoon, though, all I felt was hot fear.

Were we really meant to know?

I mark that hour's exchange with Jilligan as the beginning of my adventure into doubt. I label it the starting point, the moment when I first began to consciously admit that the blacks and the whites I'd been raised to believe were blending into an indistinct gray in my mind.

I cut class for the first time. I found myself, with Jilligan, sitting at the bottom of the staircase in the dark place where people went to smoke. There was no one blowing clouds just now, but the stench lingered. There was just Jilligan and me and this conversation we were having that was suddenly more important than going to class.

At least Jilligan seemed to think so, and I felt duty-bound to finish what we'd started.

"What's the big deal if you miss a class?" she had said. Something inside me had agreed, although another part was filled with uneasiness. I did not like to break rules.

"You have such an incredible religion," Jilligan was saying.

She had gone down to her father's office in Salt Lake on Friday afternoon. He had had a few things to finish up, so Jilligan had walked down to Temple Square for an hour or so. She had taken a tour, she said.

"I told them I was visiting from Boston. They tried to figure out what ward I was near." Jilligan laughed. "What's a ward? What a ridiculous word. It suggests mental and psychiatric and maternity."

I had thought of that too, of course, although the word was such a natural part of my vocabulary that it caused no serious flinch. Now, through the eyes of Jilligan, I thought again how awkward it was.

"What filled me most of all, though, was this wonderful sense of what a conflictless life a believer in your religion must have. I mean, everything is so clear and simple. Get a testimony of the Book of Mormon and everything will fall into place. Is that really what it's like?"

"I guess that's the basic concept."

I didn't know what to say.

It was supposed to work that way, I knew. If I knew the book was true, then all else would follow. And I had always felt that the book must be true. There was so much good in it. But if Jilligan were to ask me how I knew, what would I say?

"I couldn't really ask all the questions I wanted to," Jilligan continued. "I couldn't even think of them all at the time. It's just so amazing to stand there and realize that these people really think they have the only way to go. It's so bold. Then they show you this little book and tell you an angel revealed it to a regular old farm boy with the incredibly ordinary name of Smith." Jilligan paused, the stream of her words stopped for the moment.

"Do you really have all the answers, Katherine?"

Her question fairly took my breath away.

I stared dumbly, uncertain whether Jilligan was laughing at me or was respectful of my peculiar faith.

How I wanted to answer her, to fervently bear testimony to her of what I knew. But my mouth was gummed up; my words were jammed in my throat as if someone had stuffed old socks down it. Worst of all, my feelings couldn't work themselves clear.

But Jilligan had changed the subject anyway. Perhaps her questions were more rhetorical than literal. Or perhaps she could see I had no answers for her.

I learned of her older brother, a graduate of the Harvard Business School, who lived in New York.

And I learned that Jilligan wanted to be a doctor, although she worried that her handwriting was too neat. I listened to her excitement about medicine, her idealism, her wanting to know how everything works inside us, her desire to help heal. Her love of science was equaled by my inclination toward language, I was sure.

"I want to be a brain surgeon." She looked embarrassed, almost, as she told me. "Do you think that's funny?"

I didn't think it was funny at all. Someone had to have a dream like that, and she might as well be the one.

"I get so blown away by the intricacies of the brain. They tell us it's some spongy gray matter, but it's the very stuff we're made of." She hurried on. "I want to know how it all works. How the feeling gets put into action. How we love, hate. How the electricity up there translates into emotions. And I want to help people who have brain-related disorders."

She paused for a moment, just barely long enough to swallow, and then continued.

"And what makes some people have faith, for that matter? Maybe I'm more into psychology than into the brain, huh? Like, why did your Joseph Smith have so much capacity for belief, while others can't believe in anything but what they see? I think it's all in the brain. If we could just explore it, become involved in its intricacies. . . .

"It's only a dream now, Katherine, you understand.

Mostly I'm just trying to get As in all my science and math courses. And I read college texts, and take APs, and talk to my brother's friend who's in medical school, whenever he comes over. And I read books about the brain and the spine, and look through AMA journals when I can. I keep feeling I should be doing so much more than just that. But what can I do? I get so darn frustrated. I'm stagnant in high school when I ought to be in college. And I can't tell if anyone takes me seriously."

Jilligan shrugged, then shook her hair, swinging behind her back the long strands that framed her face.

"Does it really matter?" I said. It was a dumb response, I knew, something more to break the force of Jilligan's earnest hopes than anything else. I regretted that I'd said it, but Jilligan responded thoughtfully:

"I guess it shouldn't matter. But it does. It helps if you feel other people think you have it in you. Especially since I'm not a man."

My own mind was far away now, wondering at what she had said about the brain and faith, no longer listening to her musings.

Did our ability to believe have something to do with the kind of brain we had, the way our chemicals got together? I had never thought about it, but now I remembered a friend of my father's who had been in an almost fatal car accident. His injuries were to his head, in his brain, and the damage was irreparable. Confusion would fill him after the accident, the doctors told his wife. Gradually, though, he began to find order in his mind again, although his short-term memory was largely useless.

My father told us that since his accident his friend had lost his sense of spiritual truth. He couldn't feel the warm, right feelings anymore. He had lost his ability to feel directed by the Holy Spirit.

We had talked about it in a family home evening. My father had spoken with sorrow. He could not imagine a life without the ability to hear the Spirit speak, he had said.

24

I wanted to tell my father that I wasn't sure how the Spirit spoke to me, and I hadn't been in a terrible car accident. I wanted to tell him that I really wasn't sure how to know that the Church was true. But I didn't say anything. I felt that such an admission might hurt him. Or, worse yet, perhaps he would think it was normal.

But what about his friend? Perhaps his chemical composition had been altered, and he had lost the capacity to feel the Spirit.

Where did we feel that Spirit, anyway? Oh, where did it all come from? I was weary with the thought of it all.

I was still asking questions of myself, long, long after Jilligan had stopped talking. We had gathered up our books from the steps and walked slowly back to class. It was American History, of course, that we had chosen to intrude upon. Jilligan and I walked into Mr. Enfield's class late. He raised his eyebrows in our direction as we entered the class. I could feel his eyes following us to our seats, despite the uninterrupted pace of his lecture.

There would be no punishment for our lateness, I assumed. He would call Jilligan up after class, and she would say something right and reassuring to him, and that would be the end of it.

I dutifully enumerated the effects of the revolutionary war in my notebook. But in the deeper part of me, I was still asking a question.

What made us believe?

I found her in her backyard that afternoon, sitting on a wooden porch chair, listening to a recording of the Book of Mormon. She was in Third Nephi.

"Hello, Katherine."

"Auntie."

She motioned for me to sit, and put a finger to her lips. I listened with her, shutting my eyes and enjoying the warmth of the afternoon sun on my face, my body.

The Savior was directing the Nephites to ponder the things which they had heard and prepare their minds for the morrow. He invited those who were lame or blind or leprous or afflicted in any manner to come to him.

"Bring them hither and I will heal them, for I have compassion upon you; my bowels are filled with mercy."

Auntie turned the tape off then.

"You know, I listen to those verses whenever I start to feel sorry for myself. I think of all the thousands of blind people who have lived on the earth. To me it's a real problem, my not seeing. But people have had to deal with this kind of darkness since the beginning of time, I guess. My problems really aren't very big at all, are they?"

"Do you feel like that a lot, Auntie?"

I was embarrassed by my question as soon as I spoke it. Perhaps I had no right to know Auntie's feelings. Yet it startled me to think of Auntie as feeling sorry for herself. She seemed like the last one alive who would ever feel pity for herself or let her problems defeat her.

She seemed not to hear my question.

"Wouldn't it be wonderful, though, to have been there with Christ? To see again?"

"I guess so, Auntie."

What would it have been like, I wondered, to actually have seen Christ, to actually know Him. After talking with Jilligan that afternoon, I felt myself so much like Thomas. A great desire to visit Jerusalem filled me — to stand in the places where the Savior had stood. What I would give for that kind of trip! Surely there would be a spirit there that would speak to me loudly of Christ. Or if I went to the Sacred Grove, surely I would feel it there.

"Those beginning days of total blindness were horrible," Auntie continued, more to herself than to me. "There was no difference between day and night. Everything was black.

"I'd always been alone, you know, after Harry died. But I never felt so completely cut off from life as I did during those first months of total blindness. Not even after Harry was gone did I feel so alone."

Auntie pulled her sweater around her.

"Of course I knew it was coming. Dr. Arnold had given me enough warning that the sight in my left eye was dimming fast. He didn't have to tell me what I already knew.

"But I am proud, Katherine. I really didn't want any help from anyone. Just like after Harry died, but then I was younger by twenty years—and I could see. I could afford to think that I really didn't want anyone, not even my own daughter, or need anyone to help me too much.

"But to lose my sight completely! I was going to travel so much. I was going to go to Europe and the Middle East. I was going to take all those wonderful BYU tours."

I thought of Auntie's books, the wall full of them in her living room, the other wall in her study, with its big desk where she had graded papers year after year.

"I still remember what it was like to teach your class that year. Do you remember that year, Katherine?"

Of course I did. She knew I did.

"I wanted so much not to frighten you children. A blind old lady with a cane and all."

"It wasn't so much the cane, or that you were old, Auntie. It was getting used to the idea of your blindness. I couldn't understand it then."

"And do you understand it now?"

"Oh, Auntie. The whole wealth of what I don't understand right now could fill a book."

"You? My most valiant Top-pilot?" She laughed gently.

I told her about my conversation with Jilligan that afternoon.

"Why didn't I bear my testimony to her?" I asked Auntie. "Why did I feel such confusion fill me? And why did I have to be born in this crazy religion, anyway? It's supposed to be my great gift. It's nothing but a big burden, really, a set of regulations."

"Katherine!"

Maybe I should go totally crazy, I thought, and join the hypocrites who acted one way at home and in the ward, and another way at school.

Or I could just forget everything and exist in lonely isolation, an exile from the faith.

It wasn't that I wanted to smoke or drink or sleep around or blast Pink Floyd from my radio with the druggies. It wasn't that at all. All those options were completely impossible to me. It was just the noise in my mind that bothered me, the wanting to feel settled and right and sure, the needing to be a real Mormon. If I couldn't feel right and sure about it, I didn't want to do it.

I just wanted to be able to know, really know, that's all, that God had communicated with Joseph Smith. Was that so bad?

"But it's a wonderful religion, don't you think, Katherine?"

"What? Why?" I was startled for the moment. Who could think of my religion as wonderful?

"The way it forces us to come to terms with it. The promise it offers, that if we just ask, we'll know. But what a terrible, almost scary burden it is. You are feeling the burden of it now, aren't you, my dear?"

Auntie began to hum a Primary song quietly.

"Don't you remember it still? I can hear you there, my little Katherine, singing in your crazily loud, tuneless voice as we'd march around the classroom, the old, blind lady with her cane and her eight-year-olds in tow. You were my little angel of light that first year."

And Auntie began to sing, right there in the backyard, her old voice creaking out a shaky but correct melody:

Called to serve Him, heav'nly King of glory,
Chosen e'er to witness for his name,
Far and wide we tell the Father's story,
Far and wide his love proclaim.
Onward, ever onward, as we glory in his name;
Onward, ever onward, as we glory in his name;
Forward, pressing forward, as a triumph song we sing.
God our strength will be; press forward ever,
Called to serve our King.

I almost joined in with her, almost felt the song fill me once again. It was a rousing kind of tune, hard to resist, inviting participation. But something held me back. It was better, for the moment, to let Auntie sing alone.

"Who was that?" Krestin asked.

It was Jilligan, of course, although I had certainly never expected to see her here, not in Allen's Food Mart. I had thought she would surely buy her groceries only in Smith's, where everything was neat and orderly and new—and more expensive. But here she was, clattering noisily on the old wooden floor of the store like the rest of us, rummaging up and down the aisles, tossing food in her wagon with its inevitably wobbly wheels. Her cart was full. Amazingly, she pushed it for her mother. I had not thought she had a mother, somehow.

Jilligan's mother was a dull-looking woman with a flat face and bleached hair. She was overweight, the fleshiness clinging to her cheekbones unpleasantly. She wore a plaid housedress. I was stunned to think that this beautiful girl could have a mother so plain.

Jilligan introduced us with some embarrassment, I thought. And I introduced Krestin to them both. He held out his hand. A sweet smell lingered in the air between us, although I was unsure where it came from.

"You must be the young friend Jilligan has spoken of. I tell her to bring you over, but you know these teenagers. They don't want to do anything their mother says." She winked at us, leaning towards us confidentially. The scent came from her breath, I thought.

"Well, Mom we really ought to get going. Dad said he was going to try to be home early tonight."

"Is that right, dear? Why didn't you mention it sooner? You do so enjoy hiding things from me."

Jilligan steered the cart off, and I was left standing dumbfounded with Krestin.

"That is one beautiful girl. What hair! She sure wasn't in school when I was there."

I heard Krestin's words, but I was thinking more of Jilligan and her mother. Why had Jilligan never said anything about her to me? Then I did remember something she had said about divorce. I felt sick at the thought of it, sick that my idealistic friend with her

29

dreams of doctoring and hopes for being a surgeon should have a mother who seemed so dumpy and uninteresting. But perhaps I was being unfair. Her mother had been friendly and conversational, despite her vacant eyes.

"When did she move into Orem?"

"Didn't I tell you about her?" I asked Krestin innocently enough, although I had purposely never told him of Jilligan.

"Not that I remember. And I probably would remember. Especially if you had told me about her looks."

I felt a pang of female jealousy pierce me. Of course Jilligan was beautiful. That was why I had not told Krestin about her. Even though I had mixed feelings about being Krestin's girl, there was no point in inviting competition from Jilligan. Besides, as I had learned about her mind and her hopes I had placed less importance on the fine features of her face, the loveliness of her hair, her large, bright eyes. And I had a feeling, too, that Krestin would not appreciate the kinds of questions Jilligan had suggested in my mind.

I told Krestin about her now.

"Wow, she must really be going through some adjustments getting used to life out here. Kind of like the opposite of going on a mission. She comes to Zion instead of us going to find her. What does she think of the Church?"

"Why?" A feeling of protectiveness filled me. I didn't want Krestin to think of her as a possible convert. Not yet, anyway.

"I think she thinks it's interesting," I responded. "And I think she kind of respects us. She's been to Temple Square and all. But I don't think she's on the verge of any conversion or anything."

"Why not?"

"Because it's hard to believe it all."

Krestin looked at me head on. We had come into Allen's to buy some chips and soda to take to the BYU football game that afternoon, not to talk religion.

"What do you mean?" he asked.

"Oh, never mind."

Krestin went on about how maybe the Lord had sent her here at this critical point in her life to learn about the gospel. Maybe we would be instruments in the Lord's hands to bring about her conversion.

"This would be a great experience for me before my mission, don't you think?"

"But it's all so complex," I mumbled helplessly, more to myself than to Krestin.

How could I tell him? I thought, grabbing a bag of Fritos and three cans of soda. It was all so stupid of me anyway, and I knew it would hurt him to hear my wandering thoughts.

The problems were with me, weren't they? and not with the Church. There was something wrong with me if I felt I couldn't believe completely. Wasn't that what I had been taught? If I couldn't see the truth, then it was because I wasn't reading, I wasn't studying, I wasn't praying enough.

The Lord was always waiting on the other side of the door for my knock, wasn't He? The Church was true. It was me who wasn't.

I felt guilt for my uncertainty, my doubt. It was better not to speak of it.

But Krestin wouldn't let the subject drop. We roared up to the Marriott Center lot in his "Bug," listening to the pre-game show. They were talking about Gifford Nielsen and the mess at Arizona State. I thought Krestin had lost interest in my impulsive statement. Surely stats were more interesting to him. But as he turned off the radio and we grabbed our gear, he began his query again.

"What were you talking about back there, Kath? I just can't believe you could say a thing like that. I thought you were a real Mormon, too, not like those kids who can't make a commitment. Or the ones who ask so many darn questions. Aren't you sure?" There was gentle concern in Krestin's final question.

I was unwilling to pursue the discussion with him in the crowd of people marching toward the stadium. It would get too messy, of course, and maybe Krestin was right. Maybe I was just like the others.

I had relied on my parents' faith for so long. Everything seemed right and good. But did they really know? Maybe they were just following the path that their parents had taken.

Something snapped sharply and painfully in me at that thought. I was not willing to believe that extreme, either. Better just to wallow in indecision and confusion for a while than to pass any judgment.

The Cougars ran out onto the field. The band blasted "Rise and Shout." I sang, fumbling for the words that I was never able to remember.

It should have been a perfect autumn afternoon — endless blue sky above the Wasatch Front and temperatures in the seventies. I was sitting next to dear old Krestin, a BYU freshman, and he wanted me to be his girl. All was warm and fine and fun.

But I felt crummy, confused to the core.

Hadn't Krestin ever doubted?

The Cougars won the toss and elected to kick off. I watched them line up and held my breath as the players ran to begin the first play of the game.

4

In the dark of night, after tending a sick child or nursing the baby, I sometimes shut my eyes tight and try to find the way to my bedroom. It is more a game for me than anything else, reaching out in the blackness, trying to control the urge to open my eyes and see the familiar landmarks in our apartment—the clothes hamper in the hallway, the low bookshelves, the covers of our bed.

There is so much that can be done by instinct. Without even trying, we memorize the place in which we live just by our constant use of it.

Yet one night I stumbled on a shoe that had been left lying in the hall. I opened my eyes instantly, reaching out to steady myself, not wanting to wake the whole house with my foolishness.

How much better it is to have faith than mere belief.

"Do you think I could join your seminary class?" Jilligan asked.

I guessed that was okay, I said. There didn't seem to be any restriction requiring a member of the class to be a member of the Church. I thought it would be just fine.

Jilligan approached Mr. Enfield with her question next, a perceptive way of gaining the aid of a teacher, I thought. He was delighted to assist her with enrollment in the class, despite the fact that it was October already.

Jilligan came to be in the same seminary class as mine. Perhaps Mr. Enfield worked it out that way. I'll never know. But there she sat, her long hair flowing in front of me, just as she did in AP American History. Her graceful, slender arm with its elegant fingers was often raised, her careful comments causing a stir in the class and in my mind.

I wanted to disappear sometimes, pressed down in my chair by the weight of the noise in my head.

Could she not keep quiet? Could she not just sit back and passively take it in like the rest of us?

Only Stacey Patterson ever raised her hand in class, and that was only when Brother Turner was playing devil's advocate. It was as if we all had signed a secret pact to endure the class and its corny jokes with a minimum of questioning and concern, all of us sitting quietly in our faded Levi's. Only Stacey cared enough to offer an answer to one of his questions.

But then Jilligan began, gradually, to turn the class around. She seemed to want to know what we Mormons were about. We were new to her, and she was certainly new to us. And she had that wonderful, genuine curiosity, the kind that couldn't be condemned.

"Now, who do you believe wrote this book?" she asked.

I had to admit that it was a wonderful question, one which we all took for granted, but her asking it made most of us take note.

Brother Turner explained the origins of the Doctrine and Covenants, that the sections were revelations received by Joseph Smith directing the early Church.

"But whose voice do we read? I mean, it's not like Paul talking to the early Saints, is it? Is this the way God talks?"

There was a bit of irreverence in such a question, and I felt myself cringing, but there was no denying Jilligan's sincerity.

"I mean, if I'm a believer and I read this book, then I get to know the way God talks and thinks, don't I?"

Jilligan always spoke of God, never of Heavenly Father. Even with my adolescent skepticism, I felt a warm wonder at the way we Mormons approached "God," as Jilligan called Him. We knew Him as our Heavenly Father. How much kinder and more intimate, more reverent that was.

"Well, that must really be an incredible book to believe in then," Jilligan said.

She had that way about her, of never actually admitting to have faith herself, but of making us all feel as if we had found a wonderful thing, a pearl of great price for which we should rightfully abandon all.

We talked after the class.

"How *did* Joseph Smith get all those revelations?" Jilligan asked.

"Well," I replied, stalling for a moment, feeling a flash of almost panic pass over me. How *did* he get them?

Some were revelations from the Urim and Thummim, I said. And some were visions, and some were answers to questions that he had. And some, I said, must have come into his mind somehow. I found myself overwhelmed by her question.

How did they actually come into his mind? Did a voice speak the words into his head, somehow?

"Ask Brother Turner," I said. But Jilligan seemed not to notice my uncertain answer.

"I really don't think there's another book around that matches the claim of your Doctrine and Covenants," she continued. "Oh, I suppose there is. What do I know about all the religions of the world? But it just seems so incredible to think that God is actually speaking there. Not in a burning bush and all, or with thunder and lightning, or even on top of a mountain. But with our normal speech. Our normal English language. And it really was English, wasn't it, not some translation from something. He just spoke in regular old American English.

"Why aren't you shouting that from the rooftops, instead of always just proclaiming that the Book of Mormon is the big thing. That book is full of just regular people talking, isn't it, in translation, no less? The prophets and all, I mean? But this is the voice of God. A whole book of it."

I told her I guessed that she was right about the Book of Mormon, that it *was* mostly prophets speaking. Except, of course, for that part where the Savior visited the Nephites.

"And a prophet's voice is the same as God's, isn't it?" she asked.

"Uhmm."

"Well, maybe that *is* just Joseph Smith talking in the Doctrine and Covenants then. Maybe it's no different — just a prophet speaking in God's name. But no, some of the revelations are very clear. This is the voice of Alpha and Omega, the first and the last." Jilligan spoke those last words in a grandly deep voice. "I wonder what He really does sound like."

Jilligan was puzzled. I was trying to remember the section where the sound of the Savior's voice is described.

"I just think it's so incredible how you Mormons think God can actually speak to your prophets today. And you even believe He can reveal Himself to you, right?"

"Well," I said, feeling I was treading on dangerous and unfamiliar ground, "I know we feel the Lord can direct our paths. But I don't think Heavenly Father would reveal Himself to me. I'm just a little nothing. He would go to the prophet, first."

How bumbling it all felt in my mind. How stupid I felt!

Our conversation stayed with me throughout the day, even as I worked at school late that afternoon, editing mundane copy for the newspaper.

The construction plan for the new high school made the front page this month. I would be graduated, of course, before the first class entered the new building, so to me it seemed somewhat irrelevant, or maybe just a case of bad timing. And there was all the sports news, and the class news, and the silly editorials and opinions and letters to the editor. And there were the seminary reports.

"This month Mr. Turner's class will continue its introductory examination of Church history and of the Doctrine and Covenants," the article began. Stacey had written the story for our class, of course. It was dull and uninteresting, just like the class had been.

Until lately, of course, when, for the first time, I was beginning to reckon in a mature way with the hugeness of my faith. Was that really the voice of Jesus Christ in that book?

Jilligan was right. It was an incredible book of scripture. And an incredible religion.

Dad came home from a bishopric meeting one Tuesday night in early November and informed me that Auntie Anna wanted to meet with Mom and me and Sister Davis the next afternoon. Sister Davis was a registered nurse in our ward, and she had been taking care of Auntie's medications for years now. So after school the next day, Mom and I rang Auntie's doorbell, neither one of us quite sure what to expect.

My father had been evasive about it all. "They want to change the schedule of care we give Auntie," was all he had said.

"Hello, Katherine. Ruth," Auntie said. "Isn't it a beautiful day? I hope the winter never comes, don't you? October is such a wonderful month. I really think it's my favorite." All the talk about the weather seemed unnatural somehow, an indication of our uneasiness, of our not knowing what we had come for.

We went in and sat in her living room. Her home was always amazingly neat, partly because each week a different sister in the ward was assigned to help her clean her house, and partly because Auntie was quite fanatical, herself, about having everything kept in exactly the right place—or else she became disoriented, she said.

As Mom and Auntie talked on about the weather and the roses, my own memory relived an afternoon when I had found Auntie, in the early years of her blindness, at Cherry Hill Park. She was standing in the middle of the large playing fields waving her cane and turning herself slowly around in circles. I was in fifth grade then, and I still walked home from my elementary school every day, through the park.

"Auntie!" I called. "Are you all right?"

"Is that you, Katherine?"

"Are you all right?" I repeated.

She told me she had gotten disoriented somehow, confused, uncertain as to where she was in the park.

"Didn't they used to have a picnic bench right there?" she asked me. "And then twenty steps westward and I would find the sidewalk."

"There's no picnic bench there anymore," I told her.

The memory bothered me still, the sight of Auntie swinging her cane, lost in the familiar, simple ballfield.

My mind returned to the present with the ringing of the doorbell. Sister Davis called in a hello through the screen door. Without waiting for a response, she walked in.

We talked of the weather again, of the ward, her daughter and my brother on their missions, the hospital. And then there was a silence.

"Well," Sister Davis said, "I guess we need to discuss why we're all here today." She paused. "As we all know, Auntie has had diabetes for most of her adult life." Sister Davis coughed, then quickly added, "Well, I guess I didn't have to tell you that. I feel like I'm in a staff meeting, somehow."

We all laughed lightly together, in that self-conscious way people have of chuckling when they are uncertain and unsure of themselves.

Sister Davis continued.

"I've been in charge of monitoring Auntie's medication, measuring her blood sugar and adjusting her insulin intake appropriately, all the normal diabetic care. And Auntie, here, has been giving herself her shots, for the most part, every morning and every night. But things are getting more difficult, aren't they, Auntie? Impossible, actually." Sister Davis paused.

And in that silent moment — that prolonged and uncomfortable moment, while the voices of the children playing in the street filled the still living room — I sensed how difficult it was for Auntie to admit she needed help.

"I've been coming by at least three times a week to make sure things are going all right. But I guess we've both come to the conclusion that we need help now." There was another pointed silence. Sister Davis looked at my mother and then at me. My presence at this meeting was beginning to take meaning.

"Bishop Murphy thought you'd be willing to help, as you live right across the street. And are such good friends."

Sister Davis went on hurriedly. "We'd teach you both how to give Auntie her shots. She needs one in the morning and one at night. And you could measure her glucose level, and then report it to me. I would still make the decisions, and monitor the amount of insulin in the injections. We just need more help."

"You've been doing this all by yourselves, all these years?" my mother asked.

"We've all been working this thing through together, right, Auntie?" Sister Davis said. "After all, I've never taken her shopping or cleaned her house like you and so many of the others. It just seemed natural that I should be the one to monitor the drugs and keep in touch with Auntie's daughter about her medication. It's been my calling, more or less. And Auntie's been so independent about it all, anyway."

"But my hands are starting to shake so much lately," Auntie filled in quietly. She had been sitting silently, her hands folded in her lap. "I really am getting old, you know, although I hate to admit it. I just can't seem to manage the shots and all."

"Of course we'll help," my mother said.

Of course we would learn how to give Auntie the shots. Of course, it only made sense, since we were such close neighbors. My mother answered for both of us.

"It will be all right, won't it, Kathy?" she asked.

I was nervous, but I knew I wanted to help.

I looked at my dear Auntie Anna, sitting so quietly in

her chair. I felt pain and embarrassment radiating from her, filling the room. What would it be like to never see?

Of course I would help all I could. There was no one I wanted more to help. But the thought of putting a needle into Auntie's skin filled me with fear. A sense of dread crept over me, making me uncomfortable and restless in my seat. I stood and walked quickly across the room to the front door.

"Katherine?" Auntie called.

Krestin wanted to be a teacher when he finished college. He wanted to teach secondary ed.; I thought he would be great at it, and I told him so whenever he seemed to waver in his convictions, as he did today.

"I mean," he said, "I really wonder if it matters what we study. Suppose I just work in the 7-Eleven for the rest of my life. Your father seems happy enough. And I'd probably make more money at the 7-Eleven than I would teaching in Utah, anyway." He laughed to himself. "As long as I live a good life, raise my kids, love my dear wife dearly" —and he winked at me— "I'll be fine, won't we, Katie, my dear?"

"Katie? Ugh!"

But it wasn't the name that filled me with disgust. Wasn't there more to life than working in a 7-Eleven?

"I don't know. It's so hard to keep motivated and all. I know I'll be off on a mission in six more months. What does it really matter what I study right now? It's all going to be interrupted, anyway. It all seems kind of hopeless, doesn't it?"

"But when you get back, you just pick up where you left off."

"Wherever that might be."

I could tell Krestin wasn't convinced. He shifted gears angrily, picking up too much speed for BYU's slow limit. He thought better of it, and reduced his acceleration as drastically as he had increased it. The car lurched and belched obediently along, a slave to its confused master.

Krestin and I were growing increasingly restless with life, I thought, each in our own way. He felt the pressure of a mission filling his thoughts. And I felt the grand confusion of wanting to know everything about faith and life all at once.

Why was Auntie Anna blind? Why could Jilligan view Mormonism from a safe and fascinated distance, and I had to be right in the thick of it? Why did my family have to spend so much time being faithful? How did my little life fit into the grand scheme of things? There were so many people in the world; so many words and thoughts had been written and spoken. How was a person to know it all? The questions knocked angrily in my mind.

"I want to be good and prepared for it all, you know," Krestin continued with his mission talk. "I don't want to go out there like some jerk who doesn't know anything about his religion and who doesn't care. I really want to convert a few people to the gospel. "I know it's the Holy Spirit and all who's the real witness, but still, it can't hurt to be a prepared missionary, can it? Sometimes I just want to drop everything and go right now. Forget school and just study the scriptures. Become a fanatic for a few years. I'll never have a chance like that again."

"Uhmm," I said. In some ways he was already a fanatic, I thought.

Krestin pulled into a parking space in the law school parking lot. We walked across the overpass towards the library.

It was a perfect October evening, the stars overhead in high, bright endlessness. I loved to come down to BYU at night, to enjoy its hush, the sound of quiet talk between small groups of students as they walked with their books in hand. I saw only the purity of education on those nights, felt my mind quicken with my own desire to study and participate and to be a part of it all. It didn't matter what those students with books in their hands might be talking about. I saw only the hope for their brighter future because they were here—listening, learning, and thinking. I envied them.

I liked BYU, despite the fact that so many kids in my high school viewed it with total disgust. It was the last place on earth they wanted to go. And sometimes I joined in their tirades against it. Who would want to stay in Provo if they could go somewhere else?

But on nights like these I knew I had to start my education somewhere, and I had a feeling it was going to have to be here. My brother had gone here, before his mission, and my sister had started here too, until she got married. And I would follow the tradition. I wanted to learn as much as I could, to figure out this business of life and faith. Where better could I figure out my own faith than here?

Krestin worried about converting other people to the Church, but I was more concerned about discovering if I was converted to the Church myself. Perhaps I would find out while I was at BYU.

That was still a distance away, though. I wanted to know *now,* this year, whether the Church was true or not. But how?

We walked between the Wilkinson Center and the Harris Fine Arts Center on our way to the library. It was a good campus, I decided again, a bit new and a bit too clean, perhaps, but a very pleasant place on a clear autumn evening.

Krestin pulled me close to him. We bounced along with syncopated footsteps.

Maybe he was right. Maybe we would stick together, even after his mission was over. As long as he kept studying, stayed committed to some goal in life, maybe we would end up together. He was a pleasant sort of person, and I enjoyed being with him, for the most part. Maybe that's what made for a good marriage—just an easy sort of friendship.

Who could tell?

Maybe I could stand to be the wife of Krestin Carver, and spend my days in small happiness.

But oh! I hoped there was something more for me. Something huge and expansive and wonderful, something liberating and fine, something larger than myself.

Why did I even think that the happiness that I would find with him would be small? I wondered. Perhaps I was too much of a dreamer.

The library doors appeared before us, welcoming our entrance, swallowing our bodies and minds. The warmth from the building was pleasant. Krestin needed to go to the fourth floor. I wanted to go to the fifth. We'd meet back in two hours.

5

Sometimes, in the quiet moments of a day, I feel my testimony swell within me gracefully, powerfully. I feel it completely, overwhelmingly, joyfully. I know that life has little meaning without my knowledge of the Savior and of His prophets and of His plan for His children. I feel my mind crack with the hugeness of my faith.

But that year with Jilligan I was unable, perhaps unwilling, to sense the things of the Spirit.

Jilligan invited me to come to her house after school that afternoon. It was an unexpected invitation, one which I had thought never to receive, especially after our encounter in Allen's that Saturday afternoon before the football game. Something in me sensed that Jilligan wished to distance me from her family. Or perhaps I was the one who wished to remain separated from her home, to keep the image of Jilligan apart from the image of her mother. I know that I wanted Jilligan to think of me as being free from the encumbrances of my family, so perhaps she felt the same way.

Jilligan had mentioned Krestin, of course, the Monday following our supermarket chat, but I had said nothing of her mother. She had wanted to know all about my boyfriend, as she called him, and I had answered all her questions satisfactorily, I guessed. I wasn't sure if she approved of him or not, but I consoled myself by admitting my own uncertainty as to whether her approval really mattered. I didn't even know whether my romantic arrangement had my approval.

Jilligan lived in a surprisingly modest home. I had expected some grand Orem mansion, like the kind one of the Marriotts had for sale about four blocks from where I lived, where the old, humble part of Orem edged up closely against the new part.

Jilligan, it turned out, lived far enough away from me so that it would be quite a walk for me to go over to her house often, but close enough so that she would have been in my same stake, had she been a member of the Church.

She lived in a new raised ranch. It sat on an open, treeless lot, next to some of the orchards that had survived the developer's ax. The Mitchells had pretty views out of their living room windows. To the east were some remaining fruit trees, with the benevolent heights of Timp towering above. To the west was the silver slice of Utah Lake.

"Are your parents happy here?" I asked.

Jilligan laughed.

"My mother is happy or unhappy wherever she lives. As long as she has access to the things that make her content, nothing much matters. Her feelings aren't necessarily geographical. She rides the roller coaster no matter where we are. Anyway, she gets to go home often enough, if my dad has to go back to Boston."

I looked at her with surprise, I guess, because she continued to explain.

"She's been back three times already, now. Dad travels back and forth all the time. He's still based in Boston, even though he's out here on the job."

"What do you do when they're gone?"

"It's no big deal. They were always gone a lot at home, too. I'll probably go back with them at Christmas. I just haven't felt like being with them lately."

Jilligan brought over some soda and chips while I thought about the business of deciding when you didn't

46

want to see your parents for a while. Somehow it didn't seem quite right to me.

"Have some." She took a bunch of chips in her hand, then passed the bag to me. "Back home, my mother's always flitting around here and there. I'd just hang around the city with my friends while she was gone. Here, I read or watch TV, or go to the movies. And I walk or jog. Now that you've been to my house, I'll come over and bother you the next time they're gone, I guess. How's that?"

A thousand questions about her family and her parents marched through my head, but I stifled them. Perhaps I didn't want to know. What made her mother's happiness so mobile? Didn't she love Jilligan's father?

I thought of my own family and the way we worked. My father came home every night—tired, yes, but at least he was there. And Mom was always there. And all our attempts at prayer and scriptures. We weren't anywhere near to being a perfect family, but we did try hard to find some measure of happiness together.

"Well," Jilligan said, "let's get on to the business at hand. I wrote down some questions I think she might ask us on the test. Did you?"

We had made this rendezvous in order to study for our humanities exam. We had a big test coming up, one that I wanted desperately to do well on. It would cover the Sophocles and Plato that we'd read, the tiny taste of Greek drama and philosophy that had so moved me. The tragedies of Oedipus and Antigone were especially poignant to me.

But it was harder than I had expected to study with another person. Hard especially to study with Jilligan, because I began to realize in the competitive part of me that Jilligan was very smart not only in the sciences, but in the verbal subjects too. I had already determined that I was going to be the best in English in my grade, and I felt, with rising fear, that Jilligan might well be better in English than I.

It didn't seem to be fair that this stranger should have any chance of robbing me of my prize.

Why did she have to be so smart and pretty and free to do and say whatever she wanted?

"What kind of questions do you think she'll ask about Plato and the cave?" Jilligan asked.

"I don't know," I mumbled uncooperatively.

"Brother Turner could use some of this stuff in his D&C class. Listen to this, Kathy. Plato says that belief cannot be either ignorance or knowledge, but something in between the two." Jilligan laughed to herself, then looked over at me. I could feel her eyes puzzling over me.

"What's the matter with you, anyway, Kathy? Don't you want to do this?"

I was relieved when somehow the conversation steered to other things, like Jilligan's boyfriend back home, and Krestin, and colleges, and the ACTs and PSATs, and the Church.

Jilligan's boyfriend, Charlie, was a sophomore at Boston College. He wasn't sure what he wanted to study, she said. Right now he majored mostly in partying and women. Jilligan used words to describe him and his looks that made me uncomfortable. She asked me if I slept with Krestin.

"My goodness, no!" I blurted out, the innocence of my response making me angry.

Jilligan laughed at me. She sat back in her chair and let her smiles turn into outright glee. "How stupid of me to even ask you!" she said.

I couldn't help feeling that her question was entirely premeditated, designed to embarrass and annoy me. I wanted to wound her in return, this worldly-wise child who thought she knew so much more than me, but I didn't know how to. I surely didn't want to know anything about her relationship with Charlie.

"Don't worry," she responded laughingly, "I haven't slept with Charlie, either. You can still be my friend."

What did she mean by that, I wondered. But there wasn't time to think. Our conversation turned, abruptly, to the Church again.

"Can I ask you some more questions about your church?" Jilligan asked. "I mean, some personal kinds of questions."

"I guess."

"I mean, have you ever had a witness that it really was all true? When Brother Turner talks about that experience he had, how it was all light and warmth and joy and all—have you ever had that?"

I didn't answer. I just sat there, once again helplessly unable to respond.

"You know, I really believe he has had that happen to him, but I don't think I really believe it's because God has spoken to him. Do you think He has? Don't you think Brother Turner is just awfully good at talking himself into believing it all, that he's somewhere in between ignorance and knowledge, like Plato says?"

Her questions hurt. I'd had thoughts like hers before, sitting in fast and testimony meetings wondering how all these people knew the Church was true? And could I know? Perhaps my problem was that I lacked the courage to ask.

"Religion is so strange, don't you think, Kathy? I mean, we Catholics think we're the right ones, but it's clear to me we can't be right. And so do the Protestants. And then there are the Jews, who don't even accept Christ. Suppose they're right? And then we have you Mormons, and the way you think you're really building a kingdom right now. Not to mention all the Eastern religions. Talk about a confusing mess."

I wondered that evening all the way home. I walked along the quiet streets, avoiding the busier ones, meandering my way. How could a person ever know the truth?

And what was wrong with me? I thought. And where could I find my answers?

"Have you been over to Auntie's yet?" my mother asked.

I sat on my bed, huddled over my Doctrine and Covenants. I looked at my watch.

"Oh my goodness, no!"

"Do you want me to go over for you tonight?"

"It's okay, Mom. I just wasn't watching the time."

I went to the hall closet and put my winter coat on over my pajamas. Auntie wouldn't mind if I came casual. As a matter of fact, she wouldn't even know what I was or wasn't wearing unless I told her. It was a strange thought, almost comforting.

It was turning cold now, although we still had had no frost. I hadn't considered the cold, damp grass in my hurry to get over to Auntie's. The wetness soaked into my slippers, chilling me.

A passage from the D&C lingered in my head as I hurried along. We were still in the early part of the Doctrine and Covenants in seminary, and I was beginning to get ahead of the teacher. Brother Turner was dwelling on the history, and I found myself more interested in the scriptures, somehow, the voice of God talking, as Jilligan had called it.

I just had read those verses in section 46 about gifts, how to some it was given to know, and to others to believe on their words. What did that mean? I wondered, as I walked up the steps to Auntie's house. Maybe Brother Turner had been given a gift, then, to know, although Jilligan thought he was just gullible. And maybe I would never know, not the way I wanted to, unless I was also given the gift to know.

"Is that you, Katherine?" Auntie called. "I hope you don't mind, but I already got into my pajamas."

I laughed. She had on a pink striped nightgown. She looked so slim and fragile in it.

"You won't believe this, Auntie, but I'm in mine, too."

We laughed.

"A real pajama party here, yes?" Auntie said.

I busied myself in the kitchen, getting out the tiny bottle with the insulin in it. I tore open the needle, then inserted its point into the rubber at the top of the vial. I turned the needle upside down, pulled the plunger back to the right CC line, and checked for bubbles. It was ready now. I only needed to prepare Auntie's skin with a little alcohol. I felt the familiar hot flash fill the palms of my hands. Although my job as evening nurse was getting easier now, I still couldn't entirely control the nervousness that passed through me, the responsibility I felt for Auntie, and the great swelling of love that inevitably filled me as I took the business of her medication into my control.

Auntie waited patiently in the living room, her sleeve already pushed up, her head slightly to one side.

For two weeks we had been "in training" together, as Sister Davis called it, and then we were on our own. My mother had come with me the first few nights after the training had ended, until I finally had to admit that I really did know what to do and she might as well just stay home. If I had even the slightest doubt about what I was doing, I asked Auntie.

The first two times I was entirely on my own I couldn't get the needle in on the first "throw," as Auntie called it.

"Relax, Kathy. Don't worry about hurting me. It's like throwing a dart," she had said. And she was right.

"Bull's-eye!" she said tonight, as she often did, after the needle was in. "Good shot!"

I pushed the plunger down as evenly as I could, then withdrew the needle.

"How on earth did you ever do this by yourself all those years?"

"I'm a very determined old lady, Kathy. People who see can do it by themselves, with practice. I just needed a little more practice."

"But how did you see to fill the needle up to the right amount?"

"Sister Davis helped me. She prepared the needles in advance for awhile. Then she found a supplier who could get me some pre-measured ones." Auntie's fingers tapped on the arm rests of her chair restlessly as she spoke. "But then the blood sugar got so erratic, and she had to come so often to measure them out for me. That was too much to ask."

51

Auntie laughed her quiet laugh.

"As long as no one ever moves anything around in my home, I'm just fine. I guess if someone really wanted to drive me crazy, or drive me to an early grave, they could just come in here and move things around. Then I'd be lost."

I went back to the kitchen to dispose of the needle. As I put things back in their proper places, Auntie called in, "How's that friend of yours from Boston making out here in dull old Orem?"

I came back into the living room to answer her.

"What made you think of her?" I asked.

"Oh, nothing, really. She just entered my mind."

"I went to her house today after school. She asked me if I knew the Church was true, Auntie. She asked me some other things, too," I said with a laugh, "but let's not talk about them!"

"Uhmm. I can just imagine! And what did you say to her question about the Church?"

"Nothing."

Auntie was silent.

"What are you thinking, Auntie?"

"Just remembering how it was for me. It's not always easy to find faith, is it, Kathy? But you have such a good family. Not that the family gives you faith, but it does help. And you had so much faith as a child. The funny thing is, even when you think your testimony is alive and well, sometimes it slips from you quite without your knowing it."

"Then you *really* know, Auntie? Like the Doctrine and Covenants says, about having a gift to know?"

Auntie was silent again.

"Oh, I don't know about having a gift to know. There have been times when I could have answered your question with complete honesty and said no, I really don't know at all, not in the total sense of empirical knowledge. And I don't think there's anything wrong with that. Because there are other times when everything in me is alive with the knowledge of truth and light."

"Jilligan said something like that the other day, though I don't think she meant it to be a positive comment."

"Did she? And is she going to join our church, then, someday?"

"I don't think so, Auntie. Maybe I'm being negative, but it's hard to imagine such a change." I stood to leave, then thought of Jilligan's comments about the Doctrine and Covenants.

"Auntie, whose voice do we hear in the D&C? Jilligan asked me how we got the revelations, and I mumbled something about the Urim and Thummim and visions and stuff, and I'm sure she thought I was from another planet. How would you answer that question?"

"I probably would have just said they were revelations, and let it go at that. But as to the voice question, it *is* the Savior speaking. I could probably find you many scriptures to show you that."

Auntie paused. The hum of the fluorescent light in the kitchen suddenly filled the house with its sound. Somewhere outside, car doors slammed. Auntie spoke quietly.

"That Doctrine and Covenants is such an amazing book, isn't it, Kathy? Our most modern revelation. We can actually hear the voice of the Lord speaking there. In our day. It's wonderful."

I moved to the door. For the moment I could almost, but not quite, sense the great kingdom-building dispensation I lived in. A part of my mind shuddered and didn't want to think of it. But another part felt the great wonder of it, the miracle of discussing such things.

"Katherine?"

I paused, holding the front door open.

"Your testimony will come. Even now, living here in dull old Orem. You will see. You will study it out and you will ask and you will find truth. The grace of this church is that it promises us a right to know, to receive a witness through the Holy Spirit. That is such a marvelous concept, Kathy, don't you think, that we can all have at least one moment when we can feel the witness of the Spirit? And for some of us, we will feel truth —again and again —as long as we worthily ask."

I let myself out the front door, closing it quietly against the cold. I thought about the irony of it, the way Auntie sat there in her darkness and her blindness, promising me I would see.

The stars seemed close tonight, touchable in their endlessness and their beauty. I marvelled at the complexity of our lives —the way we were part mind, part spirit, part machine. Surely a loving Creator had formed our bodies, had given us life and choice and a plan to follow to draw us back to Him. I felt a movement within me, a sense of tumbling and of leaping, a feeling of joy, of lifting and of love —of divine love for *me*.

Like those who bow to the east, or wail at the wall, or travel to Mecca, Krestin and I made our annual pilgrimage to the mountains each October. Perhaps our fathers had instilled this seasonal longing in us. As children, either Krestin's dad or my own had taken any or all of our family members up the Timpanogos Trail each October. I had been to the top twice, walking on the loose rock at the very top of the mountain with great care, feeling a supreme sense of space and light and of the divine Creator. Perhaps that is why our fathers braved the trail so uncomplainingly with children in tow. There was a feeling at the top of that mountain that we shared without speaking.

"We've got to go up together this year, Kathy. I've just got to go one last time before I leave on my mission. I've got to have that memory fresh in my mind, because who knows where I'll be next fall. For sure I'll be without these mountains for two years."

We had decided somewhat spontaneously to go climbing. Krestin called the night before, and the next morning I scurried out in the pre-dawn darkness into the warmth of his sputtering "Bug." I threw my gear into the back seat. Krestin's small backpack was already scrunched between the back seat and the floor.

"What did you bring to eat?"

54

We both laughed. When we were little, the snacks and goodies that our mothers gave us were the only thing that kept us going. We'd barter and exchange our food packages all the way up the mountain, stopping to rest and bicker once every hour or so. Gradually, though, as we got older, we grew less concerned with food and more interested in the scenery around us. Now, as a mature old couple out on a major trek together and alone, all we seemed able to do was to reminisce.

"Did you make any of those Rice Krispie treats?" I asked.

"Did you bring the boodle box brownies?"

"Thanks so much for coming with me, Kath," Krestin said, in between our remembrances of our favorite snacks. "I should have given you more notice, I guess, but this is the only free Saturday when there isn't a home game until November. And then there'll be white stuff to contend with. So it was more or less go today or not go at all."

"I'm flexible," I said.

The sunrise began to color the sky as we passed the entrance to Sundance.

"We'll have to go home through American Fork Canyon. Then I'll have it all locked in my mind for safekeeping."

There were already four cars in the parking lot, along with a beat-up van that looked as though it held the remains of a Scout troop in it.

"No horse trailers, thank goodness."

Krestin laughed as he shifted the weight of his backpack, adjusting the straps. "Remember the time . . . "

I didn't let him finish, laughing, embarrassed by the memory.

Then Krestin stood suddenly still. He looked at me with great kindness and affection.

"Katherine Gardner, I do believe I love you, you know. I know I've never said it before, but I truly feel I do."

Krestin shook his head and looked down at the ground. I gazed up at the mountains, afraid to let my eyes meet his. It was a wonderful statement, so warm and true to everything I knew Krestin to be and to feel. It sat out there in the lovely early morning in all its beauty and simplicity, in all its innocent and deep emotion and naiveté, a statement to treasure greatly. I was embarrassed to death, but how I embraced the happiness that his words made me feel!

"Let's go, then," Krestin said, abruptly. Perhaps he had thought I would respond in kind, but my silence unnerved us both, I think. Nodding, I followed dutifully behind him.

We hoped to make the top of the mountain by lunchtime, or at least make our way to Emerald Lake. The last coloring of dawn was fading into sunlight as we started up the trail.

We said nothing for what seemed like a very long distance. The yellow aspen leaves, shimmering against the background of evergreen, the scent of autumn, the fresh, clean air, all worked their spell on me as we walked. I could imagine no time better than this, no world more beautiful to behold than this one. Life seemed effulgent with evidence of God's love, just as I had felt two nights before while crossing the street from Auntie's house. I knew Krestin shared my reverence even without my speaking my thoughts.

We stopped for a rest on a rock beside the trail.

There was something between us now, something unidentifiable that turned the casual touch of our fingertips as we exchanged treats into currents between us. Krestin had uttered his deep feelings, I knew, down at the bottom of the mountain, spontaneously and with honesty. And although I had not returned his declaration of love, my femaleness knew his pronouncement was a great treasure.

We continued up the mountain.

I was filled with a sense of great changes to come as we walked. I was aware that life was changing for us, soon, as Krestin moved on to his mission and I made the decisions about college next year. As we continued to climb, a sense of internal restlessness began to gnaw at me, the shadow of changes to come.

Krestin placed his lips gently on mine when we stopped to rest beside Emerald Lake. I had not known that a kiss could be so tender and just nice. Jilligan had wondered if I had slept with Krestin, but I had never even kissed anyone.

I had hoped, before we left the mountain, to talk to Krestin of faith and of feelings, of my questions and my wonderings, of Jilligan and of school. But instead, all thinking vanished into a kind of blurry insignificance as we climbed higher and higher. There was only this mountain, this summit to be reached. I felt a great metaphorical climb within me, a quest to understand my faith, to learn more of love, to make decisions that would determine my future, to grow up and out, to find whatever potential I had within me. And there was this movement of gratitude within me for the great and simple blessings of my life — the privilege to live and to breathe and to see and to feel and to touch.

How good life was!

6

I feel it sometimes still, in a restless moment, when I wish I had gone on and gotten my Ph.D., or when John comes home late from church assignments tired and hungry—too tired to really talk to me. I think how simple life would have been without the Church, without its responsibilities, without the great commitment it demands of us. And as I teach my sixteen-year-olds in Sunday School I feel their agitation, their longing to figure things out and get on with life—or to abandon faith and live without thought of the Church. I tell them what I tell myself in those moments—that despite our impatient spirits and twentieth-century distractions, faith is the greatest gift we can seek, the only source of meaning in an otherwise meaningless existence.

Jilligan was obsessed with worry over the PSAT/NMSQT. I had not thought much about it. It was just another one of those standardized tests that I had come to look upon with disgust. As long as I had my number two pencil and a pack of gum and could shade in the ovals fairly evenly, I couldn't do too badly. All of those tests were variations on the same theme, anyway.

"But don't you realize how important this test is?"

Actually, I had been thinking more of the BYU Homecoming dance that was scheduled for that same evening.

I did love to go to dances, and since our hike up Timp on Saturday it was clear that Krestin and I would be going together.

Jilligan was exasperated with me, I could tell. "But this test determines if you will qualify for a National Merit scholarship! My brother was a finalist and I'm going to be one too. It will sure help get me into a decent pre-med program."

Jilligan explained to me how they added up the score totals on the different parts to determine if you qualified as a nationally renowned smart person. I thought it was a pretty unfair way of trying to find the best brains.

"Suppose you get sick that day," I said.

Finally, I admitted that I guessed the tests could be pretty important, but I was going to go to BYU and live at home, and that was that. I wasn't about to worry about winning any great big scholarship. My father had already told me that I could work part-time in any 7-Eleven I wanted, and that would help to fill my bank account during the next two summers. And I could still work while I was in school. So who needed a scholarship?

"Don't you see how important it could be?"

Jilligan seemed completely exasperated with me, but the more obsessed she became with the idea of passing this test with flying colors, the more sarcastic I became about its importance.

I did care about one thing, although I had never told her. I wanted to consistently earn the highest score on all verbal tests in our grade, because I knew I wanted to teach verbal things some day. That was my only goal in high school, one that I held with great silence and determination, and I felt that I would surely succeed in my quest. But since Jilligan had moved in, her scores had always been a very close second to mine. Last week she had even beaten me on an English quiz.

It annoyed me that she said she wanted to be a doctor, and yet she had to be so good in English, too. Why couldn't she just excel in science, and leave the English to me?

60

Now, as she rhapsodized about the PSAT, I had to admit to myself that I surely didn't want her to do better on the verbal part than I did.

"For such a smart person, you sure are dumb about some things," Jilligan said hotly to me. "Don't you want to do anything serious with your life? How can you be so narrow-minded!"

I was startled by her comment. I settled down into my seat in seminary confused by her reaction. What had I done to make her so agitated? But she wasn't only upset with me. Before Brother Turner even began his lesson, Jilligan raised her hand.

I wanted to wave my arms in a sign of warning towards him, but Brother Turner, of course, was delighted at Jilligan's obviously urgent interest in the class. We were usually a terrible class on Monday mornings, half-asleep and unwilling to show the least bit of attention to his lecture. Of course Brother Turner gratefully looked forward to another one of Jilligan's intelligent comments.

"I was reading some things this weekend about the Book of Mormon," Jilligan announced. "It seems there are some probable sources that this book could have originated from."

Jilligan went on to give a summary of what she had read. Most of what she said was new to me—events that she said happened in Joseph Smith's early life that he had included in the Book of Mormon; the Indian burial grounds in New York State; the Solomon Spaulding stuff, and another book that could have been a possible source. I had heard vague suggestions of some of the controversy surrounding the Book of Mormon, but had never really gone out looking for it. I was amazed not so much by the information that Jilligan was presenting, although that was startling enough, but by the clarity of her presentation. It was as if she had rehearsed what she was now saying several times over.

Brother Turner made an attempt to interrupt or to even silence her once or twice, but he had no success. Although I suspect Jilligan thought she was performing a great service to scholarship and faith by announcing all these problems in this basic book of our faith, she did little but antagonize the class. By the time she finished her several-minutes lecture, hands were up all over the room. Brother Turner himself appeared to be distressed.

Cody Larson raised his hand and said he'd never heard a lot of that stuff before, but he had a brother on a mission, and his brother just baptized a whole family and they knew the book was true.

JanaLee Bonnett said that knowing the Book of Mormon was true wasn't dependent on logic alone. There was something else that helped you to know it was true. JanaLee said she knew it was true.

Richard Gordon said for a while he figured it would be easier not to believe, but there was just too much good in the Church to let it all go by. He was going to go on a mission as soon as he could.

Priscilla Moulton said that although there were some things we couldn't understand about the Book of Mormon, there was also so much wonderful geographical and historical evidence that showed its truthfulness.

Jason Gardner said he had prayed about it and had received a testimony that the Book of Mormon was true.

The class fairly erupted with spontaneous discussion.

Brother Turner said, finally, that the nature of the book and the way it had come forth would always lead to arguments. But for everything opponents claimed was wrong with it, there was something good that a person just knew to be true. The Church, however, was anxiously and unselfishly bringing people to Christ, and the Book of Mormon was the great foundation of that latter-day work.

After everyone who wanted to speak had spoken, there was a moment of soundlessness in the classroom, as if we were all absorbing the energy of our shared comments.

I had not said a word, of course. I was so impressed with the good sense of my classmates. I was almost amused by the amount of faith that we had managed to keep hidden from each other in our self-conscious unwillingness to speak of spiritual things. For those few moments we united ourselves in the face of Jilligan's comments. Friends who had never said a word about the Church voluntarily spoke up.

"Remember when you asked last week how the early Mormons could be so true to their faith and give up everything they had—again and again—to build Zion? And then get beaten? Just look at the way you all rallied to the support of Joseph Smith here and now. There is something in us that testifies to the truth of this church. And we defend it."

Brother Turner lectured a bit on the Kirtland period, then closed the class by bearing his testimony—not with his usual floweriness and premeditated prose, but quietly and simply. Then he publicly invited Jilligan to read the Book of Mormon too, and take Moroni's promise to heart.

As the bell rang and we gathered our books, Jilligan turned to face me.

"I guess I sure made a fool out of myself, huh? I was just so startled by what I had read this weekend, Kathy. Here I was, thinking maybe I ought to consider the possibility that your church might be true, and then I read all that stuff. It seemed to me you people needed to hear it too, and not just go on blindly assuming what you've got is true. But I didn't think I'd cause such a stir."

"Faith is hard to figure, isn't it?" I responded, more to myself than to Jilligan. "Do you think you really will read the Book of Mormon?" I added.

"Yes," she said, "I think I will." Under her breath she added, "I guess I'd better."

It was family home evening. We held it just about every week. My mother tried hard to ensure that we always had a song, a prayer, a lesson, and a snack, but some nights all we had was a snack and some meandering conversations about our life and times and faith. Now that I was the last *old* child at home, and my brothers were so much younger, it often worked out that our lessons catered more to them than to me. I missed those talks with my older brother and sister and my parents.

Tonight Mom was discussing Lehi's vision of the tree of life. We reviewed all the symbolism in his dream. Then Dad stretched masking tape through the family room in crazy patterns for the boys to follow blindfolded. Whenever they hesitated or stumbled, Dad sang out boldly, "Hold to the rod! The iron rod!"

"Come on, Kath!" Jim insisted. "You have to do it too!"

My father blindfolded me and warned me to watch out for the crowds in the large and spacious building. And then I was off, stumbling along the sticky tape, trying to find my way through the dark and dreary wilderness of our family room.

I should have told my parents about Jilligan long ago, I thought as I stumbled along, but I hadn't as yet said very much about her. I kept her in some distant other world, safely apart from my family. I should have told them about her crazy outburst in seminary this morning, about how so many of the kids had rallied to the defense of their faith, and about how I had said nothing.

"Is something wrong, Kathy?" my mother asked me for the third time.

"I'm fine," I responded, "just a little sticky in the fingertips."

I couldn't bring myself to talk with my parents about my faith. I was afraid they wouldn't understand it if I expressed even the slightest doubt. I didn't want them to think any less of me or, worse yet, run the risk of receiving some lecture I probably wouldn't want to hear. So, after successfully getting to the "tree," I poured the hot Karo mixture on the popcorn in the brown paper bag without a word, then watched as my father shook the sticky sweet mess inside the bag. I ate my treat in silence.

The house quieted down gradually. Jim and Bill went to bed, and Dad worked silently at his old beat-up desk in the corner of the family room. Mom was writing her weekly letter to my brother in Japan. I went to my room to do my homework.

There was that picture again, with its inscription: I Will See You Again. I wondered what temple it had been painted in. Or was it just on display in a visitors' center somewhere?

What would it be to know, to *really* know, to feel the nailprints, to hear Him say, "These wounds are the wounds with which I was wounded in the house of my friends"? Would knowledge make any difference?

I did some homework and then wandered over to Auntie's house for her nighttime shot.

She was happy to see me.

"I'm so glad you came over just now, Kathy. I've been sitting here feeling so blue and dark. Sometimes life seems a bit too long for me lately. I'd like to get on with the next estate and get my eyes back again."

"Auntie! How can you say that? What would I do without you?"

I couldn't imagine her gone. "Every kid in high school needs someone like you to talk to."

"Is that right?" she asked. "And every sick and blind old lady needs someone like you to talk to at night, too."

"Then it's settled," I said grandly. "You'll live forever."

"For a time, anyway, my dear." Auntie paused and rearranged her shawl around her shoulders. "My daughter wants me to come back to California, you know. She thinks I've lived long enough on my own out here. She thinks it's about time I came where she is and let her take care of me. What do you think of that, Katherine?"

I didn't like the thought of it at all. I resented her daughter for even intruding on Auntie's life. Where had she been all these years when Auntie lived and worked here alone? She hardly ever came to visit.

"My daughter has always wanted me to come and live by her, you know. She pleads with me on behalf of her children, threatening me with the thought that I will go to my grave barely known by my grandchildren. We call each other every week, too. But I have never wanted to live near her. I think it would ruin the great friendship we have."

Auntie paused.

"She's not active in the Church, you know. She went out to California with her husband after they were married because he was doing graduate work at UCLA. And they just gradually drifted from the Church. I guess I didn't want to live near her and see her not going to church all the time, even though she sends her children, thank goodness."

Auntie paused again, and a strange sort of smile passed over her lips quickly. "It is such a painful religion, don't you think, sometimes? When those we love so very dearly just can't accept the things that we know are true. The hurt seems never to go away."

I thought about Auntie's words as I prepared her insulin injection. I thought, too, about Auntie's daughter, and wondered how it was for her to reject the values she had been taught. There must be suffering on both sides when a person turns away from the Church, I decided. Suffering and awful guilt.

Auntie picked up our conversation almost as if I had never left the room.

"Just by its very nature, you know, the Church causes a sort of desperation on the part of a parent. When a child starts to wander, the parents can't help but tighten their hold on the child, wanting to force faith and a testimony upon them. I tried to do that with Marcie for years from a distance, and then I realized that she had to find her own way in life. And her father couldn't stand to see me so despairing over it all.

" 'She'll find her own way,' he'd tell me. 'Free agency is the grandest principle of the plan,' he would say.

"But the thought of going back by her now to live and to feel that sorrow again—I just don't know if I could do it. It would surely drive me to the grave."

"What about your son?"

"Oh, he's a bishop out there in California. He's fine and happy and successful. But he's a son, and he's all involved in his wife's family. Plus his job is out there. I would just never think of becoming a burden to him, and he's never asked me to live with him, anyway."

I held the needle poised, absently rubbing her arm with the alcohol pad as I wondered what I could say to lift her spirits.

"Bull's-eye!" Auntie called as I gave her the shot.

"Oh, Auntie!" I laughed. "How could you ever be a burden to anyone?"

"A blind old lady with advancing diabetes will become a burden to everyone before long. I can't see any way around that."

I waited in her living room while Auntie changed and got ready for bed. For some reason I didn't want to leave her, keenly aware of her frailties. In a wild panic of thought, I imagined her dead in the morning. My mother would find her, of course, and then she would have to come back and tell me. It was cold and awful.

I went into Auntie's study and examined her book titles while waiting for her to get ready for bed. Her library was full of English and American literature, and there were all sorts of titles to skim over.

I picked up a beat-up paperback edition of *Robinson Crusoe.* I had never read the book, yet Auntie obviously had. I began to thumb through it, skimming the yellowed pages here and there, reading sentences Auntie had underlined, smiling at her notations in the margins.

"There you are!" Auntie said, as naturally as if she could see me standing before her wall of books. "What are you looking at?"

"*Robinson Crusoe.* I can't believe the things you underlined in here. It sounds like something out of Mormonism, for sure!"

Auntie had underlined many things in the book, but my eyes caught two passages at random. One stated that we would never see the true state of our condition until it was illustrated by its contraries, nor how to know what we valued or enjoyed but by the want of it.

"And listen to this one," I said to Auntie. "It sounds like a quotation by Brigham Young that my father has taped in his scriptures.

" 'Nothing but Divine revelation can form the knowledge of Jesus Christ, and of redemption purchased for us; of a Mediator of the new covenant, and of an Intercessor at the footstool of God's throne; I say, nothing but a revelation from Heaven can form these in the soul; and that, therefore, the gospel of our Lord and Saviour Jesus Christ (I mean the Word of God), and the Spirit of God, promised for the guide and sanctifier of his people, are the absolutely necessary instructors of the souls of men in the saving knowledge of God, and the means of salvation.'

"Isn't that fantastic? When did"—and I looked at the name of the author on the cover—"when did Daniel Defoe write this?"

"In the late sixteen hundreds, I think. Or maybe early in the seventeen hundreds. I can't quite remember. But it is a wonderful book. Most people think it's just about a man shipwrecked on an island and his friend, Friday. But it is about so much more—about God and discovering and explaining the highest of philosophies. I wrote several papers on it in college, I remember. It seems something so natural to all men—to turn to their God, however they see Him to be."

"Oh, Auntie! Doesn't it all just boggle your mind? There are so many people in the world. So many things to believe in! How do we know what's right? The Church seems so much less true to me when I think that I am in it. Why should I have been given the truth? Surely with all the people in the world there are others more deserving to be in my place!"

Auntie laughed—a gentle kind of chuckle.

"Katherine! You are so good to hear. I think you are a wonderful young woman, so preoccupied with yourself and your thoughts. Enjoy this time to doubt and to wonder and to question. But there will come a time when you will have to follow Crusoe's advice—and seek a testimony by the power of revelation."

Auntie found her chair at the desk.

"Do you know, I have been thinking about your question—about the voice in the Doctrine and Covenants. I found a scripture for you to read. Are my scriptures on the desk? Here, I think?" She paused, finding them, then giving them to me. "Let's see now, I was listening to my tapes when I heard it, but I think I typed down the reference on my machine there. It was in D&C 18, I remember."

I looked over the paper that was still in Auntie's typewriter.

"Here it is. D&C 18:34–36."

"Read it, Katherine."

I found the reference.

" 'These words are not of men nor of man, but of me; wherefore, you shall testify they are of me and not of man;

" 'For it is my voice which speaketh them unto you; for they are given by my Spirit unto you, and by my power you can read them one to another; . . .

" 'Wherefore, you can testify that you have heard my voice, and know my words.' "

"What does that say to you, Katherine?"

"That it *is* the voice of the Lord in the D&C."

The thought that Christ had spoken all those words filled me with wonderment.

"Yes," Auntie responded. "Isn't it spectacular to think that?"

"But Jilligan would still want to know the details of how all those words came to be. How did they get into the mind of Joseph Smith? she would say."

"And you?"

"Sometimes I want to know, too."

"You will come to understand things, Katherine. Keep thinking, keep looking for your answers. Like our friend Crusoe, you will find them."

Auntie had to get to bed, I knew. I followed her into her bedroom, turning lights off as we went. After she was safely in bed, I moved to turn the bedroom light off.

"Leave it on, dear, would you please?" she said. "I decided to leave a light on in the bedroom in case something happens to me in the night and I have to call someone for help. I want my rescuers to be able to see where they're going in the dark."

I walked back across Auntie's yard with a great heaviness in my head. The black sky with its dots of light stretched out in limitless immensity above me. I thought of Kolob and of worlds without end, of the sea of glass and fire and of the Urim and Thummim and of my own tiny and insignificant soul. I thought of life and of death and of the great loss of hope that must come with death when there is no thought for a life beyond. I thought of Auntie and her daughter and of Jilligan and her attack in seminary and of Brother Turner and my parents and my brother in Japan. I thought of Krestin, too.

Despite my restless confusion, I felt a sense of joy stir within my mind. How grand life was with all its complexities, with all of us struggling in our many different ways to find our answers and reasons to be.

I turned the doorknob, then looked back at Auntie's house. The light glowed from her bedroom window.

Our climb up Timp changed things between Krestin and myself. Until then, we had never acknowledged any deep feeling between us. Sure, we called ourselves boyfriend and girlfriend and enjoyed the status and peace it gave to our lives, but we were not in the least bit passionate. Krestin joked casually about how we would marry and raise kids, and I thought of how it might be to share his name, but I never considered what he was saying or what I was thinking very seriously. Yet Krestin's statement of love and his kiss had caused a difference. I felt a sure obligation within me that I would have to kiss him again now, that once we had started declaring our love, we would have to continue it. There was a feeling of happiness in the thought, but also one of fear and entrapment. I was only sixteen.

Krestin had come to our ward for church today. We sat together dutifully. He reached to hold my hand. It was incredible that we should display our feelings publicly in sacrament meeting. Any of our friends might see us and surely they would wonder why all of a sudden

Krestin and I were holding hands. It would cause a stir, I was sure.

No one said anything, of course, but I was sure everyone who saw us was at least thinking something, and probably even laughing at us. My little brothers certainly were. I heard Bill whisper to Krestin, loudly enough for me to hear, "Take your hands off my big sister, you goop!" Krestin blushed, redness inching up his neck, infusing his face with a rosy hue. The blushing made everything worse for me. My hand started to sweat in his. My fingers began to cramp.

When the meeting ended and we got up to leave, I felt a sweet relief. But my father whispered in my ear as he headed off to a meeting in the bishop's office, "Amazing how the onslaught of a mission call makes a young man's heart turn to thoughts of love, isn't it?" He laughed gleefully at his joke.

How could he have seen Krestin and me holding hands from all the way up on the stand? I wondered mournfully. Everyone must have seen us, for sure. It was a terribly embarrassing thought.

But after church, in the comfort of home, with Krestin slapping cold cuts onto a roll, I thought perhaps it would be pleasant to be in love with him. He was, after all, a likable guy, easy to look at and often fun to be with.

"So I'll pick you up at about eleven for the football game next Saturday, okay?"

"Eleven?" I said.

"It starts earlier because it's Homecoming."

"But I've got to take the PSAT this Saturday, and the test won't be over till twelve."

"Well, I guess you'll just have to skip the test. I mean, what's more important," Krestin asked with mock heroics, "football or another stupid test?"

"Football!" Jim and Bill answered together gleefully as they entered the kitchen.

"You got it, guys! Revenge! Maybe they'll even see the light and let my good buddy Giff toss the ball again!" Krestin shouted, jumping up from his seat at the kitchen table and tackling my brothers on the floor. "Nothing matters more than the warm sun and the green grass and the Cougars!"

Jim and Bill and Kres untangled themselves and stood to sing a sickly version of "Rise and Shout." My sandwich tasted like paste in my mouth.

Their tuneless song resounded again in my head that night as I finished up some last-minute homework.

What really was more important? I wondered. I had already expressed to Jilligan my disgust with the test. Perhaps if I didn't show up it would convince her once and for all that I wasn't as devoted a student as she. She had been at me again this week, after the seminary discussion, urging me to talk more in class and to say what I was thinking. She wanted me to forget about BYU and to try for some other schools.

"Why do you allow your religion to run your life so much?" she had asked.

I hated her for asking, for confusing me, for making me think those thoughts. Maybe she was right. Maybe I should think of doing something else in life. Maybe her entrance in my life was a blessing to get me to think more about what was really important. Maybe the Church wasn't true. Robinson Crusoe certainly knew about God and the Holy Spirit and revelation, years before Joseph Smith ever was born. Wasn't that enough?

I felt a flash of panic pass through me at the heresy of my thought.

How could the Church *not* be true?

I called Krestin later that night.

"I'm so glad you called." His voice was warm, even in his simple greeting. "I was just sitting here thinking of you. I was watching the movie about the First Vision again with my little sister, keeping the Sabbath day holy, and all. I was wishing you were here so we could share all these feelings together. I love you, Katherine."

There it was again. How could he say so easily that he loved me? Why didn't I ever feel that uncluttered spontaneity of feeling in return?

And how could we really love one another, anyway? We were so young. I didn't want to be bothered with love right now.

But my mother had loved my father in high school, deeply and surely. Perhaps I had to try harder.

"I decided not to take the PSAT, Krestin. I'll meet you at eleven for the game."

"Good for you!" he responded. "That's great. What difference would another old test make, anyway? You'll go to BYU no matter what, right? So who cares? Besides, this may well be the greatest year in BYU's history, if Nielsen plays against Air Force like he did against the Lobos. It was a regular privilege to be there for that Friday night conference game, didn't you think?"

"It was a great game, Kres, I have to admit." Nielsen had taken to the air in a spectacular way, giving BYU its first win of the season.

I opened my mouth to tell him more—to say what Jilligan had said to me about how important that test was, about how it could set me up as a very smart person in the eyes of the whole country—but I said nothing.

I wasn't a smart person, anyway. And if I was going to love Krestin and be his girl and support him before he left on his mission and be there when he came back, I might as well go to the game with him. Besides, I had always wanted to go to Homecoming at BYU—to the game and the dance. And this year was BYU's centennial year. It had all sounded so glamorous last year when Stacey had talked about it. It could only be better this year.

I wondered what Jilligan would say to me, though, when she found out I had forfeited my chance to be labeled a smart person for the sake of a football game?

I didn't want to know.

7

If I could have seen the future that year, I would have known to relax. I would have known that my life would go on, regardless of tests or of friends or even of death. I would have known that I would reach my goals, that I would have four wonderful years at BYU and two more in graduate school, that I would spend a semester in Israel, and would meet a good man to love, that children would come, and so would a mature and sustaining faith. Yet engulfed as I was by the tension of the present, every decision, every change, seemed heavy and painful, uncertain and critical.

I was surprised to see Jilligan at my door. Several times I had thought of inviting her over, but something always held me back—that uneasiness I felt about having her actually meet my family and see my home.

We had gotten out of school early, and so I had not seen much of Jilligan today. She had been in seminary, of course. She had read at random a few sections of the D&C, yet she still hadn't gotten a sense that this was a book of scripture. She thought it was interesting, but not convincing.

The whole class was involved in her searching now.

Stacey Patterson had officially lost her ranking as the only pious goody-goody of the class. Now, most everyone seemed to have something to say that bordered on the religious side.

It was good, I had decided just that morning, that Jilligan was here, because she stimulated so much discussion in our class.

"Come on in," I said, as she stood before me on our doorstep.

"Surprised?" she asked.

"I guess I am." I couldn't hide my feelings. "How did you know where I lived?"

Jilligan had asked some kids at school how to get here.

"All this east, west, north, south business makes sense to you, but it sure is crazy to me. But I got here without too much trouble. My mother hasn't been feeling too good lately," Jilligan added, "and I just didn't feel like going home for a whole dull afternoon once again."

"Don't you have any friends over there?"

"Not really. I don't go to church every Sunday like you all do. And I don't go to all your dances and activities during the week. I'm just kind of by myself a lot. I wish my father had never made me come out here for school this year!"

I was surprised at Jilligan's strong comment. I had been thinking only of my own feelings all along, of how difficult it was for *me* to get used to *her* being here. I had never thought about how strange it was for Jilligan to get used to all of us.

"I could have just stayed home and been a lot happier, but he wanted to 'broaden my horizons,' he said. And get me away from Charlie, most of all, I think."

I was embarrassed. Here I had been, half-despising her for all the conflict she had enlarged in my own head, wishing that she had never come to Utah, and assuming all the while that she was happy asking her probing questions in seminary.

But maybe Jilligan was miserable here. Maybe her interest in me really was just to have a friend. Maybe I was wrong those times when I wished I had never met her, when I wished she weren't here to tell me how smart she thought I was and how I was wasting my life away in just being a Mormon.

I had thought she took some kind of gleeful pleasure in causing added grief in my life. All she really needed was a friend, just as she had said that very first day.

"This is Jilligan," I told my mother, "Jilligan Mitchell. She's the girl from Boston I told you about."

My mother stared at me blankly for a moment, then smiled.

"Girl from Boston?"

A pause.

"Oh, yes," my mother said.

But I knew she didn't know at all.

"Well, I can see I've sure made a great impression on your daughter, here, if she's barely even mentioned me to you."

My mother stared at Jilligan.

"Well, a lot of things tend to go on around here, you know," my mother said. "Sometimes I can't remember what's been said. What beautiful hair you have!" she added.

"I'm sure that's so," Jilligan replied. "About the remembering business, I mean. I guess I forget that you all live here all the time. You're used to seeing those mountains out your window every morning. You're not here on an endurance test, the way I am. It's hard to imagine anyone really living here and having a whole life going on."

"Well," my mother responded, this time chuckling, "there are thousands of us who manage to do it quite well. Even out here in Utah. It must be a job to wash all that hair."

She invited Jilligan into the kitchen for a snack.

"What a lovely kitchen!" Jilligan exclaimed. "It's so warm and homey. Just like a kitchen is supposed to be."

I sat down in my usual spot and tipped my chair back, looking anew at the room where I had had countless meals and snacks and arguments with my brothers and sisters and tripped over toys and caught my mother and father kissing. It wasn't any great place to me, although it certainly had that well-used appearance about it. Was Jilligan laughing at us or was she genuine?

"You like the fingerprints on the wall then?" my mother responded, half-chuckling to herself. "I think they add a nice, homey touch to this old room, don't you?" She smiled to herself, then added thoughtfully: "You know, there's something about kids' fingerprints, Jilligan. Even Fantastik doesn't seem to take them all the way off. They'll stay there forever, I tell Kathy's dad, to remind us of all the little people that used to live here."

My mother paused, looking over the dim, black smudges beneath the windowsill. "I just can't get rid of them all somehow. Not that I really want to, I suppose.

"What a silly thing to talk about," she added, shaking her head quickly. My mother turned to her dishes then, rinsing them and loading them in the dishwasher. And it did seem an odd thing to talk about — yet important too, somehow.

Jilligan and I looked at the collection of faded fingerprints. I could feel myself a pre-schooler again, grubby-handed, waiting at the window for my daddy to come home, fighting with my brother and sister for the best place to stand and see.

"Maybe they're like all those things in life that we think we could have done without, and yet we can't erase," Jilligan said.

"Maybe," my mother responded. "So much for philosophical gibberish."

"So much for fingerprints," Jilligan agreed.

My mother offered Jilligan cookies and milk. Everything that was apparently normal about my life now took on a strange abnormality. I wondered what Jilligan was thinking about everything. Would she describe my family as simple, humble Mormons, and as nothing else?

It was not the fact that Jilligan was from Boston or even that she wasn't a Mormon that bothered me. It was just some element of her personality that troubled me. I realized that there was something about her that made me embarrassed about myself, that kept me wondering whether she really liked me for me or not.

"So have you always been a member of the Church?" Jilligan asked my mother.

Mom nodded.

"What's it like to be raised out here, Mrs. Gardner, so surrounded by your church?"

I wanted to tell Jilligan to be quiet, to leave my mother alone, to talk more of our kitchen, and less of our Church. I couldn't tell if Jilligan was sincere or whether she was making fun.

My mother seemed not to mind.

"Well, it's been quite nice really. I love it here. My family has lived here since Brigham Young brought the early Saints out."

"And you have a testimony?"

My mother looked directly at Jilligan.

"Yes, I do have a testimony, Jilligan," was all she said. I would have given anything to read my mother's thoughts. There was something about Jilligan that seemed to put the other person on the defensive.

"That's really wonderful to hear, Mrs. Gardner. I'm so glad you said that."

Jilligan stayed almost until dinnertime. She and my mother laughed together in the kitchen, talking of Mormons and Easterners and Westerners and a lot about faith.

"Don't you think it's pathetic that your daughter isn't going to take the PSAT?" Jilligan asked my mother.

I had talked to Auntie Anna about my decision at some length, but I had said very little about it to my mother. I held my breath, wondering what my mother would say.

"I guess Katherine has something else she'd rather do."

I became an observer. Occasionally I felt a measure of tension in the air, as if there was a potential for Jilligan to lapse suddenly into derision of my mother, or for my mother to condemn Jilligan as completely ignorant of spiritual things. But for the most part, there seemed to be peace and respect.

"Hasn't Kathy ever told you about Auntie Anna?" my mother asked Jilligan. "You mean you don't know she's been giving her insulin for over a month now?"

How funny it was to see the different paths the conversation took. I became aware that I spoke of selected things with certain people. When those different people got together, I ran the risk of having my life spill out in common disarray.

"Your daughter has her doubts about her religion here, don't you know, Mrs. Gardner?"

I held my breath again, but my mother took all things in stride. "That's quite a normal part of growing up, don't you think, Jilligan? She'll work it through eventually. One way or the other."

It was an altogether interesting scene, I decided.

On the one hand stood my mother, so quiet and faithful and devoted to principles of charity and faith and kindness, who believed so fully and completely in the goodness of our Heavenly Father and in the truth of His gospel.

On the other hand there was Jilligan, a stranger to our faith, perhaps a stranger to any type of faith, one who seemed devoted to achievement in school and in the choice of her life's profession. She was wearing her ERA T-shirt, which prompted yet another discussion.

"Do you really think men and women are equal?" my mother asked.

"Of course."

"In every way?"

And somewhere in the middle I sat, a product of my family's faith, raised as a child in the sweet and loving environment of my home, silently listening, silently questioning.

But even if Jilligan hadn't entered my life, I would have asked questions, I knew, eventually. It was, as my mother had said, a part of my growing up.

"The peas are at three o'clock, the meat's at six, and the broccoli's between eight and twelve, Auntie," my father said. "And there's a salad in a satellite dish at about eleven o'clock," he added.

"Thank you, David," Auntie replied. "That is such a wonderful gimmick. It's saved me from making a complete mess of myself countless times. It puts a wonderful mental image of it all in my mind." Auntie laughed. "Isn't it silly how wistful one can become over a dinner plate? Just to see those little peas again would be such a relief."

"Don't you hate not being able to see?" Bill asked Auntie.

"Well, yes, I do, Billy, I really do, but let that be our little secret, okay?"

"Why? You're allowed to say that it's lousy. Plenty of stuff is lousy."

"But if I say it's lousy to be blind, and I really let it get to me, then I might as well say it's lousy to be alive. And then where would I be?"

"With Heavenly Father," Jim responded happily.

"Well, yes, I suppose that's not a bad option at that!" We all laughed.

Auntie was not doing well lately. Her sugar level was strangely erratic, despite an increasingly limited diet. Sister Davis was concerned. And winter, with all its accompanying cold and "white stuff," as she called it, would make Auntie a complete prisoner in the darkness of her house.

My father was making arrangements for her to go out to dinner five nights a week at various members' homes to help ease the monotony and loneliness. Tuesday night was our night.

"You know, David," Auntie said between a careful spoonful of peas, "I do think it's about time I swallowed my old bony pride and went to live with my daughter. What do you think?"

There was silence at the table. Only the sound of Bill's fork interrupted the stillness.

"Well," my father spoke slowly, "I think we'd miss you a great deal. You're more or less a part of our family, you know, not to mention the ward family."

"My roots do go back so far here. My little house, the

81

high school. So many years here. But Marcie keeps telling me about the balmy southern California weather. And my own grandchildren, of course. It's been foolish for me to stay away so long, don't you think? Why I know Katherine here so very much better than my own children."

"Then you're not asking," my father said.

"No, I guess I'm not. I'm simply stating my decision for the first time out loud. With great fear and trepidation. How can I leave everything I've known for so long? And I'll never be back, David, will I?"

"Oh, Auntie, you can't leave!" I blurted out.

How could life go on without her? What would I do if I didn't have her to talk to? I wanted her to come to my high school graduation, to my graduation from college, to the temple with me, to my wedding. I wanted her always to be there.

"Well that's a little bit selfish," my father said quietly. "We have to let her do what's best, Kathy."

"Excuse me," I said. I left the table and went to my bedroom, closing my door behind me, locking out the world and its sharp facts.

How could Auntie leave? She had to live forever. We had said that she would. How could I ever get through all the mazes in my head without her there to steady me? Was it really selfish of me to love her so?

Eventually the tinkling and clanking of the dinner dishes stopped. Only the muffled sounds of voices filtered down the hallway. Eventually, even those stopped. Then I could hear the soft steps of Auntie shuffling down the hallway. I could imagine her hand brushing the wall as she took her slow and careful steps. I heard her hand brush my door before she knocked.

"Come in."

"Where's your bed, dear?" she asked. I took her by the elbow and helped her to get settled. Then she put her arms around me and we hugged each other for a long time. I held on with all the passion of my heart.

"How I love you, Auntie Anna!"

"It's so nice to be loved so much by you," she said, after we had stopped our hugging. "But I'm just an old lady now, Katherine. I've lived a very good life here, but I need to go home to that daughter of mine. She said the other day that I've hurt her a great deal by staying away so long. I had never thought of that, you know. I had never realized that maybe that's what I had been trying to do all along, to hurt her because she hurt me.

"I must go back and reconcile myself with her. She was such a beautiful and good daughter, Katherine. Rather like you are to your mother. Can you understand how deeply the love between a mother and her daughter goes? Perhaps someday you will know."

Auntie paused, stroking my bedspread, feeling its quilted bumpiness with her wrinkled and veined and spotted hands.

"I should not have stayed away so long. And if I die without being near her once again, without loving my grandchildren . . ." Auntie's voice trailed off, her questions unanswered. "How stupid of me!" she continued. "I have been too proud, staying away for so long. And I simply cannot live by myself any longer." The matter was settled, I knew.

I cried that night, lost in my huge adolescent ache of knowing I would surely lose my beloved friend.

She would move away, of course. She had to. I understood that. But I would remain behind, never going over at night to speak with her again, never sitting in the warm sun of her backyard, never holding her hard elbow inside her sweater. All the places that had been hers would loudly announce her absence to me.

And she would die someday, too, and I would not be there to weep at her funeral. We would just get a phone call or a card, perhaps, from Marcie, announcing the death of my dear, dear friend.

I had felt that if I just talked to Auntie long enough, she would give me the answers to life's questions, that if I could only tap the wisdom of her experience I would be free from the noise in my head. But now she would be gone. I would be alone.

In my own selfishness, I couldn't imagine life ever being happy again without her there to talk to. I did not want to grow up without her.

"Honey?" my mother's soft voice called quietly at the door. "Can I come in?"

"Oh, Mom," I said with tears. "I don't want to hurt like this."

"I know," my mother said, gathering me within her embrace in the darkness of my room.

"We'll have one good, last Christmas with her, Kathy, and then she must go home to her family. It's best. They need her. They really do. And she needs them."

It felt so good to wrap my arms around my mother.

University Avenue was lined with people who had come to watch the Homecoming Parade. This year's parade was special, too, because 1975 was also BYU's centennial. Our own Orem High band marched by, and Krestin cheered wildly, even jumping up and down on the side so he would be sure to be noticed. Stacey did see us, and managed a difficult wave while still playing her flute.

Parades, for some reason, had a teary effect on me. I was easily stirred by the music and the marching and the celebration of it all. I hid my problem bravely, though, turning my head away from Krestin whenever I felt the unwelcome wetness filling my eyes. It was a silly annoyance, this crying at parades.

"That was sure a fun one," Krestin was saying now, as we walked back to his "Bug." "Now if Edwards can just get wise and play Nielsen again. Just give him a chance. Keep throwing that ball. Maybe we can get some momentum going and clobber Air Force."

I only partially heard Krestin's words. Right at this very moment, I was thinking, Jilligan was busy scratching the blackness of her pencil into little oval shapes, determining once and for all whether or not she was a nationally renowned, truly smart person. And here I was, along with the band members in the parade, celebrating BYU's Homecoming, missing my chance to taste success.

We brought our lunch with us, courtesy of my dear mother. We drove down to the park by Utah Lake, spread out a blanket, and watched the ducks watch us eat. It was a little chilly, even with the noonday sun. Krestin moved close to me. It was pleasant to feel his warmth near me.

The football game was just as he had hoped. Edwards did play Nielsen, and BYU won with room to spare. Krestin screamed himself hoarse.

"Go Cougs!"

Krestin assured me I was seeing history in the making. "I've never seen them so good. If they can just keep this up, they'll have another winning season like Sheide's!"

It *was* exciting, although I was certainly not as screamy about it as Kres.

"It figures I've got to go on my mission next year! Now I'm going to miss two years of this. Talk about making a sacrifice!" He laughed at his own jokes. His exuberance was infectious.

When we got home, Jim and Bill came running from the house to tackle us.

"Go Cougs!"

"Weren't they great?"

Mom told us how they had been running in and out of the house to listen to the game all afternoon, even though she was sure they understood little of it. "When I told them that we won, though, they understood that!"

"Isn't it great?" Krestin said to my brothers, picking Billy up and flinging him above his shoulders. "Maybe we'll start winning for a while."

All this celebration over football was suddenly monotonous.

My brothers had already talked Krestin into taking them down to the park with him. He seemed to naturally think I would want to go with him, but I declined.

"I've got to get ready for tonight," I said.

"Women! Can you believe it, boys? Your sister is going to turn down an opportunity to play in the park with you because she's got to get prettied up for tonight."

Jim and Bill let out appropriate groans. Then off the three of them went, although it was already late in the afternoon.

"Did you have a fun time?" Mom asked, as we walked together back into the house.

"Fun enough," I said.

"Jilligan called before, by the way. She's quite a gal, isn't she, Kathy? She took that test today. I really think she called just to make you feel bad that you didn't take it. I told her I thought you were probably having a great time with Krestin and had probably forgotten all about that dumb old thing."

"It did cross my mind. But I couldn't do both, could I? Well, I'd better start showering. I really feel like lying down a little bit, too. Maybe until dinner."

Krestin came to pick me up about eight-thirty. He had even borrowed his father's car. He pinned a corsage on me carefully, joking over the fact that someone ought to invent a better pin for such occasions. His hands smelled of aftershave.

It was a wonderful night, dancing and dancing and dancing in the Wilkinson Center ballroom. There was no one who would know me there, and I felt so happy in my anonymity. I could pretend I was madly in love with Krestin and enjoy myself to the fullest. And I did.

When we got home, Krestin jumped out of the car and hurried around to open my door. Then he walked me up the path to the front steps.

"Your father sure does have a knack for gardening, doesn't he?" I could tell Krestin was suddenly nervous, finding in my father's chrysanthemums something to say to break the silence.

"You know, Kathy, today I thought it was unfair that I'd have to give up football for two years. Well, not unfair really — that's a dumb word to use — but just kind of disappointing, I guess. But now I think it's unfair to have to miss *you* for two years. At least I'm not going to Vietnam, or something like that, right? Just a few years older and I'm sure I would've been there."

Krestin kissed me goodnight. Then he ran down the walk to his car.

"Thanks for a wonderful evening!" he called back softly.

Across the street, Auntie's light glowed from her bedroom window.

8

All adolescents grow up in historical time periods, in years when events of major importance appear on the national and world scene. My high school years covered the span that included the withdrawal of the United States from Vietnam, followed by the swift and almost uncontested Communist offensive there. Simultaneously, the cancerous growth of Watergate spread, followed by Nixon's necessary resignation. Kissinger struggled ineffectually to make peace in the Middle East. Brezhnev was the somber force in Russia, and Gerald Ford attempted to reassert a shaky America as a force for good in the world. Harold B. Lee died, and Spencer W. Kimball became our new prophet, seer, and revelator.

All these events affected me only in periphery—in snatches of conversation I'd hear from my parents, or as a flash on the TV news, or sometimes as I sat down to read about them in Time. For I was too bogged down in the business of my own selfhood—of trying to figure out who I was, and what I believed in—to pay attention to the changing world around me.

I suppose that is the great blessing and perhaps, in this free nation, the great danger of our adolescence —to have the right to turn inward and explore with uncontested freedom who we shall be in the years to come.

The test results came back, of course, as they always do. My homeroom teacher announced their return with great glee.

"Today we will return the results of the PSAT/NMSQT tests most of you took several weeks ago — near the end of October, actually. And a few of your classmates will go home to have a very, *very* happy Thanksgiving, I'm sure."

Mrs. Gordon handed out the papers to each person. They were white, nondescript sheets of paper with computer printing on them. There was the usual silence as they were distributed, then the hushed voices of comparative discussions.

"Did you all get one now?"

Mrs. Gordon surveyed the desktops.

"Katherine? Didn't I give you one?"

I shook my head. "I didn't take the test," I told her, watching as her eyebrows arched.

"Why ever not?" she asked. I let her question hang in the air as if it were rhetorical. To my relief, I was truly saved from any more of her inquiries on the subject by the ringing of the dismissal bell.

Stacey Patterson, who was also in my homeroom, conferred with me on the way out the door.

"Do you think we really should have taken it?"

"I guess we'll never know, will we?"

We walked together to Mr. Enfield's room, our first-period class on Wednesdays. He was buzzing around the classroom, inquiring, I could hear, about our test results. When Jilligan entered the room, he fairly seized on her bookbag in his eagerness to know how well she had done. I listened to their conversation from my seat. But it was obvious, even without their words, that Jilligan was as pleased as she could possibly be.

"Class! Here's the first National Merit Scholarship finalist I've been able to find so far. Isn't it thrilling? And not a bit surprising, either, I might add!"

What a curious man Mr. Enfield was to me — tall and slender, balding, with mischievously bright eyes! He loved to teach, I knew, although perhaps he had been

90

teaching the same things for a little too long. He even made me feel, though, in his obvious delight for Jilligan, a sense of my own happiness for her, too. And then great feelings of jealousy and regret filled me.

Jilligan sat down in front of me as usual, her hair swishing majestically behind her. She settled her books on her desk, then turned around to smile at me, her honey-gold tresses making a greater flourish than normal, I thought.

"I did it!" she said.

"I know."

And I knew I would never forget it.

After class, on the way to our lockers, Jilligan babbled happily about her success.

"I'm just so glad I did this. Now when I go home at Christmas I can tell Charlie. He'll be so happy. I can say to him, 'See, I told you men and women are equal. I'm just as smart as you.' It'll be so fun.

"I'm sorry you didn't take the test, Katherine," she went on. "I really am. But don't say I didn't warn you how important it was to take it. I bet you would have been a finalist too, if you had just given yourself half a chance. Oh well, I guess you'll just go to your old BYU no matter what, anyway, like you've been saying all along. So I guess it's really not that big a deal. But Harvard will sure take better notice of me now, I think.

"Oh! Kathy! Maybe I *really* will get to med school some day. Do you think?"

She was so full of overflowing conversation and hope for her future. My reactions passed swiftly from jealousy to regret and landed finally, and perhaps incredibly, on a sense of happiness for her.

It *was* good that she had done it. It was great for her. She wanted to go to Harvard, and there was certainly no hope for me ever to go there. And she did want to do wonderful things with her intelligence. So she might as well taste success in her tests.

But oh! perhaps I really should have taken it too.

At least there was one good thing in my not taking it—I could go on believing that had I bothered to be tested, I might have done as well as or better than Jilligan.

I might have done worse, too.

"Kathy, would you go over and get Auntie?"

It was Auntie's night to come to our house for dinner. I had been reading my D&C assignment for tomorrow. I was up to section 93. Although I'd heard it quoted to me before in church, and I'd probably read it once or twice before, I was amazed by my reading this time. I felt a quickening inside my head, a sense of wonder at the beauty of the words and their meaning. The verses seemed to speak to me.

"Man was also in the beginning with God. Intelligence, or the light of truth, was not created or made, neither indeed can be. All truth is independent in that sphere in which God has placed it, to act for itself, as all intelligence also; otherwise there is no existence. Behold, here is the agency of man, and here is the condemnation of man; because that which was from the beginning is plainly manifest unto them, and they receive not the light. And every man whose spirit receiveth not the light is under condemnation."

"Oh, Mom!" I said to her as she stood in the doorway to my room. "This is such an incredible book. Such strong stuff!"

"I hate to interrupt you, Kathy, but I really need you to go get Auntie. She'll need extra attention crossing the street in this snow, so you be very careful with her. Mike and Suzanne are busy with the boys getting the tree ready for decorating, or else I would have sent them over to get her. She'll be so glad to see them again."

My sister and her husband had come home for Christmas. And Suzanne had startled us with the happy announcement of her pregnancy.

"We don't have an awful lot of money for gifts this year, so we thought we'd give you a grandchild instead," Mike had said.

"I'm so glad," my father replied, his voice full, even in his brief response.

I was so happy to hear the news.

A baby?

"It's due in May," Suzanne said.

Now, as I grabbed my coat and went over to meet Auntie, I wondered if I would be able to keep the secret to myself.

"Auntie!" I called, opening her front door.

I got no answer, but heard sounds coming from her bedroom. Auntie was on her hands and knees, groping around on the floor.

"Auntie?" I said, softly this time, unsure if she had heard me the first time, and not wanting to startle her.

"Is that you, Katherine? I can't seem to find my rubbers here. I know I had a pair of galoshes last winter, and now they seem to have vanished. It's still a little sloppy out there, isn't it?"

Auntie continued to rummage around.

"I tell you, if things get changed in here a bit, I'm lost."

"I'll look for them," I said. "You get up and sit here in this chair."

It was obviously difficult for Auntie to get up. I assisted her as quickly as I could.

"Oh, Kathy, I'm so glad Marcie is coming soon. I just don't want to live alone anymore. All of a sudden I feel as if my bones are not able to bend at all. And I'm forgetting so many things. It's just not good anymore."

We hobbled across the street together, Auntie and I. She was lost in her winter coat. I felt myself so young and supple and smooth.

As we walked to the front door, I warned Auntie that Suzanne and Mike were here.

"They wanted to surprise you," I started to explain.

"Oh, I'm so glad you told me they were here, Kathy dear. I'm getting too old for surprises anymore. No need to kill me off just yet!"

Auntie would be surprised enough, I knew, simply by the announcement of Suzanne's pregnancy.

And she was delighted.

We all decorated the tree together after dinner — Mike and Suzanne, Mom and Dad, Jim and Billy and Auntie. Only my brother was missing.

"Only four days until Christmas, Billy," Jim said.

We decorated the tree while Auntie sat on the couch, watching us put the ornaments on, but seeing nothing.

"That side looks a little empty over there, don't you think?" Auntie called to my father.

He had to agree.

"Now how did you know that?" he asked, smiling at her.

"I just know," Auntie said. And she smiled to herself.

I knew that sooner or later Krestin and Jilligan would have to meet, and not just for a brief moment in Allen's Food Mart. I felt their two forces in my life marching steadily toward one another. A collision was inevitable.

Jilligan had offered to stay late with me in the newspaper office, helping to read the final drafts of copy for the January issue. With Christmas intervening we had to get the copy ready weeks in advance. And the paper was terribly boring and vague because of it. Still, as copy editor it was my job to make sure everything was ready to go to the printer on the last day before school break. That was only two days away now.

"How do we get home when we're all done with this?" Jilligan asked, as we approached the bottom of the pile of typewritten pages. "Do we just walk? There sure is alot of snow coming down now."

"I'll call my mom and ask her to pick us up."

But when we left the building and walked to the parking lot, it was Krestin's car that awaited our arrival, and not my mother's.

"Jilligan, Krestin; Krestin, Jilligan," I said as Krestin got out of the car and opened the door and helped us pull the front seat up. For some reason I impulsively got in the back seat, and Jilligan ended up beside Krestin. The snow was stuck all over us.

"It sure has been coming down while we've been inside," Jilligan said. She talked as if we all knew one another well. "There must be three inches on the ground already, and we were only in there for an hour. I can't believe it."

"That's why your mom asked me to come and get you, Kathy. She figured I'd enjoy bugging around in the snow. But I didn't know I'd have two passengers to bring safely home."

"This is quite a car you've got here, Krestin."

"I like it quite a bit myself."

"Kind of irreverent for a nice Mormon boy, though."

"Do you think so?" Krestin seemed genuinely astonished. "I never thought of it that way. It's just kind of fun and cute."

Now it was Krestin's turn to start the conversation.

"So how are you making out here in old Zion? I guess it's pretty different from life back there in Beantown."

"As a matter of fact, there's hardly anything that seems the same to me."

"Is that right? I more or less thought that people were pretty much the same wherever you went. What's so different about here?"

"I guess I feel as though it's pretty hard for me to fit in, not being a member of your church, and all."

"But you've picked the nicest girl in the high school to be your best friend, haven't you?"

Krestin winked at me in the rear view mirror.

"Besides," Krestin went on, "not being a member of the Church is a relatively easy thing to fix."

"Is that right?" Jilligan said. "How come Katherine never made a suggestion like that to me? She seems to think it's a pretty challenging business to believe in. Isn't that right, Katherine?"

I had no chance to respond, because Krestin continued the conversation quickly.

"Well, that's the first I've ever heard about it," he said. "Why, Katherine is one of the smartest and truest girls in my ward."

"She is, is she?"

"What's going on here, Jilligan? Do you know something I don't know?" Krestin asked.

In the silence, I could feel Krestin's eyes on me in the rear view mirror. We were stopped at a traffic light outside the University Mall. A couple of missionaries ran across the intersection. The snowfall made them look comical as they ran, as if they were underneath a strobe light, their arms and legs moving erratically. A young mother with twins in a double stroller hurried along behind them, struggling in the snow to beat the light.

"Guess they ought to make snow tires for those buggies," Krestin said, chuckling at his own corny joke.

I had not ventured even a mention to Krestin about my doubts since my long ago attempt on the way to the football game back in September. I reserved my troublesome meanderings for my journal, or perhaps for Auntie Anna. I had never even told Krestin of the discussions in our seminary class.

No future young missionary, bright and eager as he was, needed to hear my selfish questionings. Besides, I was afraid he would react mostly with anger, and only lightly with sympathy. Some people allowed you to express doubt, or fear of doubt. But with others, like my parents and Krestin, I didn't want to run the risk of expressing such feelings.

Krestin didn't let the issue die. In between Jilligan's directions to her house, she filled him in on all her latest readings in Mormon-doubting material. I listened to it all again. Some of it I recognized as pretty flimsy, but some of it gave me pause.

I knew others knew the Church to be true. I knew the deep faith of my parents, and of Krestin, and of so many others. I felt terrible about my wavering feelings, but still they were there.

"What makes you think your church is true, anyway, Krestin? How can you think you know something as important as that?" Jilligan asked.

We were on her street now.

"It's the house right over there," I said.

Krestin turned his car into the driveway.

"What makes me know it's true?" he asked. "Religion is a huge thing, don't you think, Jilligan? I feel almost that you'll laugh at me if I tell you the single moment when I felt a difference come over my heart. You won't laugh, will you?"

"I don't think so, Krestin. Try me."

"I grew up in the Church and all. My family's as true blue as you can get. My father instilled in me his great love for the Lord. I learned very early on how deeply he knew that God existed and loved us. It made a great impression on me. Can you understand that?"

"It's hard to imagine," Jilligan said. "I guess the only thing my father has instilled in me is a desire to excel in my schoolwork so I can get to Harvard and into medical school and on my way to being a doctor."

"Well, there's nothing wrong with that," Krestin responded. "I sometimes wish my father had instilled a little more of that kind of thinking into me, too."

"But is that the reason you know, just because your father knew?"

"No. But growing up with a man like that did make a considerable difference in my life. It made me want to know too."

Krestin paused. The snow had already covered the front and back windows of his "Bug," enclosing us in our own muffled little world. It was cozy — the white snow on the windows and the evening darkness outside.

"We learned the Book of Mormon stories in my family the way other kids learn fairy tales. We used to sit and read them on the couch. And then we acted them out all the time. I was Nephi, Moroni, Ammon. I lopped off arms with the best of them. Do you know that story, Jilligan, about the arm-lopper?"

Krestin didn't wait for an answer.

"And then in high school, after I really got into seminary, I began to think it was time for me to find out for myself if I knew the book was true, and if I could stand on my own. I wanted to be able to say that I knew, even if for some awful reason my father's faith suddenly failed. I wanted to feel my testimony independent of his."

"And did you?"

"Yes. I did. I do."

"But how can a person know something like that, something so based on immaterial things? How can you make a claim like that?"

Krestin was quiet for a moment. I longed to hear his

answer as much as Jilligan did. I was glad for his easy way, his nonjudgmental conversation with Jilligan. It didn't matter to him that she asked difficult questions, or that you could tell she wouldn't understand his response entirely. He didn't know what she had said in seminary or to me. All he knew of her was this moment in the car.

"I guess you have to first study everything out. Then you have to humble yourself. You have to be really ready to ask. And then you ask the Lord. You pray to Him. You fast. You pray again. You get real hungry to know the answer. Then you get ready to hear the answer. And then it comes."

"But how?"

"For me, it came as a feeling of deep peace, an incredible warming sensation filling my whole body and soul. It was a tangible, touchable feeling. Absolutely real. I had prayed to know, and then this wonderful witness that I could actually feel poured over me. That was enough for me. I could not deny that it happened. That was the Holy Spirit."

"But maybe you talked yourself into it."

Krestin was quiet. I could tell he was honestly considering her challenge.

"No. I think not, Jilligan. The Spirit speaks to us somewhere beyond our mind, beyond thought, where only our heart can go. The only way a man can really know of things divine is by the spirit of revelation through the Holy Spirit. Joseph Smith said that. I've even got it written down in my scriptures. And I know he's right."

Krestin continued. "There has to be a moment when we let go and allow the Spirit to bear its witness to us. That's happened to me, you know. I can't deny that experience. Since then, I've just built on that initial feeling by studying and more studying and by service. And I've received so many more witnesses. There's a part of us that is spiritual, Jilligan. It's beyond the two-plus-two side of us. It's where we learn the eternal things of life."

Jilligan said nothing.

"And now I'll go on a mission to try and do some good there, too. It's a great and endless work we're involved in, Jilligan—to bring people to Christ."

Krestin's voice had become quiet, almost hushed. There was a feeling in the car of steadfastness and strength.

Now even the side windows were covered with snow. The whiteness created a soft blanket over us, binding us together in an intimate space where emotions could be exchanged.

Jilligan moved to leave.

"I guess I'd better go," she said quietly.

She got the door open.

"Thanks," she said.

She shut the door gently, afraid, I felt, to break the spell that filled the car.

Krestin dropped me off in front of my house. I struggled with the front seat, trying to push it up so I could climb out, but it was impossible to get out without opening the door first. So Krestin got out and went around to open the door for me, then helped me push the passenger's seat forward. We had said nothing to each other since dropping Jilligan off.

Now, as I stood in front of him in the snowfall, I wanted to thank him for his testimony to Jilligan.

"I do love you, Katherine, even with all your crazy questions and your wanting to always fight the truth. When you're ready, you'll ask. And you'll know, too."

I stood in the snowfall and watched as he drove away, shifting noisily down the street.

Half of me loved him. The other half hated him for being so sure that I would know that everything was true. I felt like I was a little child and he was my daddy. Still, I hoped with my whole soul that he was right.

Despite whatever happened to us, I hoped that when I finally did ask, I would get my answer, too.

At least I recognized it soon would be time to ask.

9

Who can lack faith at Christmastime?

"I was so impressed by what Krestin said the other day in the car," Jilligan was saying, as we stuffed our clothes in our lockers and got ready for gym. "He really made me think about spiritual things."

Jilligan zipped her green gym suit. Although the rest of us wore blue, she insisted on wearing the green suit from her high school in Boston.

"It shouldn't be that important, Mrs. Russell," she had told our instructor in the beginning of the term. "After all, I'm not going to be here that long. Why should I have to get another suit just so the color matches?"

Mrs. Russell had given in reluctantly. The final effect was that Jilligan always looked different — better, in fact. The green suit set off her hair. And somehow she looked more slender and athletic in green than the rest of us did in blue. But maybe it was because she *was* more slender and athletic than the rest of us.

She was better than her peers in almost everything she did.

"I had a book at home about the mind, and I went home and began to look through it after hearing Krestin talk about those feelings. I began to wonder if there was a part of the brain that had been set aside as the spiritual receptor or something.

"It seems that the argument about the difference between the brain and the mind goes all the way back to Plato and Aristotle. Aristotle saw the mind as somehow separate from the brain, and Plato saw the brain as the place where the mind operates. The book says we're more Platonically inclined nowadays, seeing the brain and the mind as essentially the same, but as much as I read and skimmed nobody ever said anything about faith. I got the impression that they felt faith was caused by the environment you grew up in."

This was no ordinary phys. ed. conversation.

"Because Krestin had been taught by his father and had heard of his father's spiritual experiences, he was able to feel his own. What do you think of that?"

It was a good question. I had thought of it already — something like the brainwashing idea. Was our faith a product of the family we belonged to?

It was time for our warm-ups, and so we stopped talking. But I continued to think about Jilligan's query as I counted one-two, one-two.

Of course, so much of what we believed was based on our environment. Had I been born in darkest Peru, along with Paddington Bear, I would probably not even have heard of the Savior, much less of Mormonism. Surely my own parents had taught me what I knew. And yet to argue from that direction was to argue impossibilities.

I *was* here and now, and I *had* been taught the gospel, and people around me proclaimed their deep faith in it. People were healed by the power of the priesthood. Prophets had seen Heavenly Father and Christ. Miracles had happened. I could not deny those events.

Faith filtered in and out of my thoughts for the rest of the day, yet Jilligan seemed to have forgotten her discussion when we met after school in the newspaper office.

"I'm kind of in a hurry, but I just wanted to stop in and say good-bye for Christmas, Kathy. We'll be leaving tonight for Boston. Maybe if I get real lucky I'll be able to convince my dad to let me stay there for the rest of the year. But if I fail, I'll see you in January."

She gave me a hug, then turned to leave the office.

"Tell Krestin I'll be reading the Book of Mormon on the plane on the way home. Maybe I'll get a feeling the way he did, something real and tangible like he talked about. Then I'll try to figure out what part of the brain it all comes from. Have a good Christmas, Kathy!"

"You too, Jilligan!" I called. I could not tell, once again, whether her quest was sincere or merely a joke.

My goodness, I thought as I finished up the last of the business for the paper. That girl sure has made a difference in my life.

You'd better come back, Jilligan Mitchell, I thought, my feelings more a threat than a challenge. You'd better come back and finish what you started.

I knew that Auntie's daughter was coming to visit during the Christmas break to help her pack, but still I was surprised to find her there. I had gone over as I did every night to give Auntie her shot. But when I rang the doorbell and opened the door as I usually did, I heard the fast and steady footsteps of someone who was surely not Auntie Anna.

"Hello," a slender and elegant woman greeted me. She was beautiful, actually, with shoulder-length hair full of curls and a long and delicate face. "You must be Katherine."

"Well, yes. Yes, I am." It slowly registered in my mind that this was Auntie's daughter.

"I'm so glad to meet you. I've heard so much about you from Mother over the years. I almost feel as if I know you."

My reaction to Marcie was quite different. To me she was a stranger, someone I didn't care to know very well, someone who had suddenly appeared in Auntie's life to take her away and who really didn't belong. She was probably interested in Auntie's inheritance, I thought bitterly, although I knew my thought was absurd.

No, Marcie was only interested in Auntie. Finally, I thought, after years of honoring her wishes to be by herself here in Orem.

"I guess I'll have to take your place as the giver of the shots," Marcie said with a smile. "You've certainly been such a help. I don't know if I would have been willing to give some old lady her shots every night when I was in high school."

"Auntie isn't some old lady. She's such a good friend."

"You two certainly do love one another, don't you." It was a statement, not a question, and I left it like that.

I felt uncomfortable being in Auntie's house with her daughter there. I was an unnecessary presence, and I hurried to excuse myself to go back home. But Marcie wouldn't let me go.

"Don't be silly. Do you think that just because I'm here everything's different? I want to get to know you too. Please stay for a while and talk. Even though I know you see me as the villain," she added, "taking *Auntie Anna,* as you call her, away from you."

I could tell there would be no escaping. Besides, it was Friday evening, without a threat of any schoolwork hanging over my head. And I did at least owe myself the right to befriend Auntie's daughter.

We settled down in the living room—Marcie, and Auntie, and myself. I could tell that Marcie had already begun work packing Auntie's things. There were boxes standing in the bedroom.

"We've barely begun. I just got in this morning. On the way down from Salt Lake I stopped at a store or two to collect boxes. It's not really that terrible a task to get Mother ready to go. She's so streamlined anyway. Mostly books, and they're easily shipped."

Auntie laughed. "A person who can't see can't afford to have much clutter around, can she?"

We talked about high school. Marcie had gone to school in Orem too, although then there were far fewer people in the valley. Now there are so many high schools, she said.

After high school she had gone to BYU and studied English. And she had met her husband, married, and then moved off to California with him. She never wanted to come back to Utah to live.

"I think there are just some people like that," Marcie said, when I asked why. "Some people love their roots so much that they can't bear the thought of leaving them. Others just enjoy the freedom of being away from everything that home represented. It wasn't that I was so terribly rebellious as a teenager, was I, Mother?"

Auntie shook her head.

"It's just that I was always restless. Restless in my mind, I guess. When Gary finished up his doctorate and got the offer to teach at UCLA, we were overjoyed. How could anything so wonderful happen to us, we thought. And so we've stayed out there, not without a few frustrations now and then. But we've been very happy there."

"Far from Zion," Auntie said quietly.

"There's no accounting for who the Spirit will bear its witness to, is there, Momma?"

All conversation ceased. It wasn't that the room had become tense. It was hard to explain just what had happened, but suddenly I felt some great gulf open wide before us, enlarging the distance between Auntie and Marcie, pressing the walls urgently outward. I wanted almost to push the space between them back together again, to heal whatever division existed.

I knew then, quite suddenly, that Auntie did have to go back with Marcie, and that my love for Auntie was no cause to make her stay.

"Want to help me pack some things in the basement, Katherine?"

Marcie stood abruptly, folding her arms in front of her as she stood.

"Sure."

It had been a long time since I had been in Auntie's basement, though once or twice I had gone below searching for a misplaced shovel or tool, or to borrow from her food storage.

"I remember my father digging this basement out," Marcie said, "bucketful by bucketful, carrying out the endless mounds of dirt and dumping them in our neighbor's pickup. I used to think it was all so futile and stupid. When Dad died of a heart attack I wasn't surprised. But at least he finished his basement. I guess Momma got some use out of it, anyway, for a while. Life can be so horribly sad, can't it, Katherine?"

We worked silently for a while. Auntie had a great deal of food storage in the basement. Most of the canned goods Marcie had decided to give away, but the dried and dehydrated foodstuff needed to be sorted and packed.

"You'd think the world was about to end if you came down into this basement, wouldn't you?"

Marcie laughed.

Although I had no right or reason to, I abruptly asked Marcie the question that was burning in my head.

"Why don't you believe, Marcie? Why aren't you an active member of the Church?"

"An active member of the Church?" Marcie laughed. "That good old label. As if activity is always equated with a good life. No, I guess I'm not an active member of the Church. But it isn't that I haven't tried. I've done some fasting and reading and praying—and some despairing, too, although you don't often get much credit for that." Marcie paused in her packing.

"Why is it, Katherine, that some people know, and others just don't? Maybe my husband and I got too influenced by our own thoughts after we left BYU. Maybe it was too easy to slip, with nobody watching us. Maybe we just needed to set ourselves free from it all. My husband was suffocating under it.

"But I'm sure those all sound like dumb excuses to you. Maybe I'm just not one of the valiant ones. Maybe deep down I simply don't care enough to know. Maybe I'm not worthy enough to know. I can't really explain it fully, Katherine.

"My brother finds great happiness in the church. And heaven knows it is my mother's mainstay. But I am the black sheep, I guess. Every family needs one to pray and fret over, don't you think?"

I liked Marcie very much, I decided, liked her honesty and her confusion and her faith. For I knew she had faith, although she seemed not to think so. And I pitied her sorrow, the submerged and painful river of uncertainty that ran beneath the surface of her words. I had been wading in that same river lately.

"Kathy?" she said, stopping from her packing again. "Is it okay to call you Kathy? Don't you think that faith is some kind of a gift, at times? Some people have it given to them, and they accept it. Others of us just don't get it, or maybe we don't recognize it when we've got it, and we just let it die. If you ever get to know, Kathy, really know, even for a split second, cling to that feeling. Cling to it with all your might."

I left Auntie's house close to midnight. We had fairly well packed up the entire basement. Auntie had dozed off in her chair upstairs while we worked. I offered to help Marcie get Auntie into her bed, but she declined.

"No, Kathy, it'll be all right. We're going to be living together now. In just a few days she'll be with me all the time. I'm so glad she's coming back with me."

Marcie hugged me at the front door.

"Come back tomorrow, if you like."

"Thanks. I will."

I turned to walk down the path, and then thought to call back, "She likes you to leave the light on in her bedroom at night, in case something happens."

"I will."

My own mother had left the lights on above the front door for me, too, I noticed, as I crossed the street into our driveway. I would not much longer be taking this path.

Krestin stood outside the front door, holding in his arms an enormous box brightly wrapped in Santa Claus Christmas paper. I flushed with surprise. Christmas had come and gone three days ago. What was he doing here today?

"Merry Christmas, dear one," he said quietly. He reached his head over the top of his large present to give me a kiss.

"Who's that for?" Billy called as he saw Krestin enter the living room.

"Who do you think it's for?"

"Well, it might be for me," Bill replied hopefully, his voice lifting at the end of his thought. "No," he added more soberly, "I guess it's not for me."

"Let's go into the family room," Krestin said, "where we might at least have half a chance of being alone." He looked pointedly at Bill.

Krestin presented the gift to me as we settled ourselves on the couch.

"Open it," he said.

I wanted simply to admire it for a moment, to enjoy the crisp folds and the enormous bow on his gift. It was a beautifully wrapped package.

"Open it," he said once again.

I opened the box cautiously, wanting to preserve the paper. Inside the box was another box, though, wrapped with equal skill. And inside that box was another, only this one had one word written on top of it.

Brazil.

I looked at the word thoughtfully for a moment, wondering what it meant, and then I fairly shouted, "You got it! I can't believe it! You got it!"

Krestin laughed and hugged me and said, "Can you believe it? I've finally grown a foot or two! It came this morning. I didn't think they'd be mailing out these things during the holidays, but there it was, "Dear Elder Carver" and all. Brazil, no less! *Fala português, senhorita?*"

"But there's more to open there, too, Kathy," Krestin said, when we stopped laughing and marvelling.

"More?"

I opened the box with *Brazil* on it, and inside that one found a very small package. I knew, of course, that something significant was wrapped inside that tiny box, obviously a jewelry box of some sort. I feared to open it, afraid that something terribly committing might be in there.

"Open it," Krestin said.

And so I did. And inside was a lovely necklace with a tiny emerald on it.

"Do you like it?" Krestin asked.

"It's beautiful." And it was. It was simple and small and, best of all, non-committing.

"There's a card, too, but I forgot to put it inside the box." Krestin laughed. "I got all wrapped up in my wrapping, so to speak, and I forgot to put the darn card in there too. Here it is," he added, pulling a tiny card from his back pocket. "Hope you don't mind that I more or less sat on it on the way over here."

In his fine, even printing it said, "Hope you'll still be there for me in May of '78."

"That's when I'll be back, Katherine. I bet you thought I gave you the emerald because it's your birthstone. But I gave it to you 'cause that's when I'll probably be back.

"Besides," Krestin said with a grin, "even if you're not here when I get back, at least you'd be more likely to keep the necklace in memory of me if it was your birthstone."

"Krestin." I said his name quietly. And I didn't know what else to say.

Would I still be waiting for him when he got home? And if I were, would we still be the same people? It was too hard to tell.

"Thank you," I said. "But I have nothing for you."

"That's all right. I never gave you a Christmas gift before, anyway, so why should you have one for me?"

Jim and Bill came barging into the room, unable to allow us our privacy any longer.

"What'd he get you? What'd he get you?"

"Bra-zil?" Jim said slowly, carefully reading the word on the wrapping paper I had removed and set on the coffee table. "Neat!" He ran out of the family room yelling, "Mom! Krestin's going to Brazil on his mission!"

"Smart kid," Krestin said to Billy. "And who is this old stranger?" Krestin said, standing politely as my sister came in the room.

"I forgot to tell you, Suzanne and Mike got in last week."

Suzanne gave Krestin a hug.

109

"Good to see you again, Suzanne. Well, my goodness, and you've got one on the way, too," Krestin said, noticing my sister's roomy blouse. "I guess I'm not supposed to say things like that!"

"It's getting a little apparent, isn't it?" my brother-in-law agreed. "These things have their way of happening."

My mother invited Krestin to stay for dinner.

"I really thought you'd show up on Christmas day, Krestin."

"I planned to, Sister Gardner, but I got kind of busy with my own family, this being the last Christmas home and all."

Around the dinner table, the talk was of missions. My family, even my sister, was only mildly interested in his gift, the business of waiting for missionaries being what it was. The main interest was his mission call.

My brother-in-law had been to Portugal on his mission.

"The language is the same, I think, but the climate is different!"

And Krestin wanted to hear the latest news from Robert in Japan.

After dinner, Krestin banged out Christmas songs on the piano. When the dishes were done we all joined together for a more reverent song-fest.

As I sat next to Krestin, hearing the mixed voices of my family singing, I wondered what all that nonsense was that Jilligan was talking about—the stuff about families and environment and faith?

There was so much joy in being in our family—tangible, real joy. I decided I'd better stop analyzing things and appreciate my life for what it was.

How could I ever have thought otherwise?

10

I existed in a landscape for that year, too. There were straight streets, meeting at right angles, numbered precisely north, west, east, and south. And there were gardens and neat lawns. And we met the school bus at the corner of 1910 and 543. The mountains were there, too—white-peaked after the snow, like sheets softly folded, or brown-green in the spring, or dry brown in the summer. And there was endless sky above. I took all those scenes for granted until I moved to dense and gray Chicago, in search of more education and, although I didn't know it then, my husband.

The seasons changed during that junior year of high school. I was aware of it, I know, because I must have chosen different clothes accordingly. But in my memory, those changes were insignificant.

What mattered was the landscape of the mind—the cerebral hemispheres, the lobes, the medulla and cerebellum, the thalamus and the hypothalamus, the limbic system.

In memory, this is where I spent most of my time.

Jilligan came back. I had half hoped that perhaps she wouldn't, that perhaps I would never see her again in my high school. I had thought that perhaps she *would* convince her father to allow her to go back to school out there. For I had to agree with her complaint. Why did she have to come out here to live for just a year? Why did she have to stir everything up in my life for a year?

We were still in the same gym and seminary classes, it turned out, though our new schedules were completely different otherwise. She would have to brave Mr. Enfield's lectures alone. I was somewhat relieved to be mostly rid of her in school. For some reason, I felt that I had to separate my own feelings from those she was helping to put in my head.

I liked her. I didn't like her. I wanted to do better than she did, but I didn't want to have to compete with her, either. I wanted to hear all her thoughts and questions, and yet I didn't want to have them become part of me.

She was so happy to see me again, it seemed, meeting me that Tuesday in the locker room for our first gym class. We talked as we changed into our gym clothes.

"We just got in late last night. I can't believe I even made it to school. I'm still feeling the effects of it all." There we stood in green and blue again.

"There's no way I could ever have come back here if I didn't at least have you for a friend, Katherine. I almost convinced my father to just let me stay home, but he insisted that I might as well finish up what I'd started. I guess he thinks it's good for me to be out here in this conservative environment. He likes Mormons."

Here she goes again, I thought. Get ready for another onslaught about Mormonism.

"It's just so different out there, Katherine. I was so relieved to be back with my old friends; I even got drunk once or twice. That's sure something you've never done, I guess."

I started to defend myself. I wanted to tell her that there were plenty of Mormons who got drunk, that there were quite a few in our class who lived a pretty rowdy life, that we weren't all blindly tunneling ourselves down some predetermined path. But why should I hold up that behavior as some sort of virtue to Jilligan? She had a way of spinning my head so quickly around that I lost sense of what was what.

"Charlie wants me to move in with him this summer when I get back. Can you believe that? My father would sure have a fit over that. But he's never around anyway, and my mother might as well be gone. As long as she's got a bottle or two she's easily duped."

I didn't want to know any more about Jilligan's life or about her boyfriend or her family. I just wanted to think of her in my own way—as someone who was smart and decent but who came from a set of circumstances that were different from mine.

Jilligan said she had seen two sets of Mormon missionaries while she was back in Boston.

"I almost stopped them to say hello, but then I figured I'd be back here soon enough with all the Mormons."

I told Jilligan that Krestin had gotten his mission call to Brazil. She seemed surprised.

"But what will you do without him? I mean, you two are pretty close, aren't you?"

I guessed we were, I said. "But life has a way of going on, mission or not."

"Do you think you'll marry him someday?" Jilligan asked.

I opened my mouth to say no, to say that we were two fundamentally different types of people, that I had to ask questions while Krestin could just believe, but I said nothing.

Maybe I *would* marry him.

Who was I to know?

"I started to read your Book of Mormon on the way home, like I said I would, but it bogged down for me. It's hard to get used to all those names. And then I got involved in a conversation about the Celtics with the man next to me, and that was the end of that. I really tried not to think about you Mormons while I was home."

I gave a final tug on my shoelaces and we headed toward the gym, Jilligan's hair swinging along in front of me. But she turned just as we got there and said with a smile, "Brazil, huh? For two whole years!"

The volleyball season had started in gym, and I looked forward to socking the ball over the net once again. Our ward had won the stake tournament last year, and I was pretty good at the game. Jilligan, it turned out, was a fan of volleyball too. When Mrs. Russell split the class up into teams for the tournament, Jilligan and I ended up on different teams.

There was opposition in all things, I thought grimly, as I trudged back to my locker after gym. It was clear that Jilligan was a serious competitor on the volleyball court, just as she was everywhere else. She wasn't there for fun. I'd have to play against her there, too.

We dressed without speaking.

"I'll see you in the newspaper office after school, okay?" she said, as she gathered up her books and shut her locker.

"Uhmm," I said.

Did she have to keep coming *there,* too, I thought mournfully. Why couldn't I be left alone?

I had been over to Auntie's several times during the Christmas break, visiting with Marcie sometimes, helping her pack, or just spending time with Auntie. She would be leaving on Saturday—now four days away. My mother and father would be driving her to the airport.

Marcie had already left three days ago. She was a teacher and had to get back to California to start the new term. And her children were home with her husband. She missed them. Besides, she had quickly accomplished all she had needed to do here—packing Auntie, arranging for the shipping of her things, visiting with old friends, learning how to handle Auntie's medications.

Marcie was a smart and beautiful woman. I had come to admire her very much, very quickly.

"Whatever happened to that friend of yours from Boston? Did she make it back after Christmas?" Auntie asked, as we sat together on the couch in her living room. Everything was boxed all around us. And what had not been packed for shipping, Auntie had given away. My mother had wanted her to come and sleep with us since her house was now so barren, but Auntie insisted that it didn't matter one bit where she slept.

Everything looks just the same to me, she told my mother.

I filled Auntie in on most of the important events with Jilligan of late—all her various theories on religion, and the mysteries concerning her family relationships. Auntie had already heard enough about the NMSQT business.

"Don't worry about tests so much," she had told me with a twinkle in her eye. "There's always another chance to prove how smart you are."

"Are you still so affected by all her questions?" Auntie asked, continuing her queries about Jilligan. "Are you still feeling somehow inferior to her?"

"Sometimes I do, Auntie, although lately I've begun to feel kind of . . ." I struggled to find the words, "I guess kind of frustrated by it all. She just keeps picking on things, Auntie. She told Brother Turner way back when that she would read the Book of Mormon and she told the same thing to Krestin. And she never did any of that. And yet she keeps picking on things.

"Actually, when I really stop to think about it, I guess I notice that there's been a change in her since she got back from Christmas."

"Maybe going home refires all the feelings of how different her life is from yours," Auntie said.

"I don't know what it is, Auntie. When she was with Krestin and me that day before Christmas, I really thought she might make a move to seriously study the Church. There was such a nice feeling in the car then. I'm sure she felt it."

"And what about you, dear Katherine? Will you go on through life like my own Marcie, asking questions but never being satisfied with your answers?"

I did not respond. All at once I was filled with the realization that Auntie was leaving, that I would most likely never see her again, and that our conversations together would end.

"Oh, Auntie! I'll miss you so much!"

I never answered her question.

"How did Jilligan make out with the Book of Mormon?" Krestin asked.

He stood to put another log in our woodstove, and then came back to sit beside me. "Did she ever do anything about it?"

"She said she started it, but it was all kind of strange to her."

Krestin wasn't in school anymore. With only seven weeks until he entered the LTM, he was trying to earn a little bit more money for the two years to come. He worked days at a 7-Eleven in North Orem, subbing until my father could find someone to manage the store. This was the second night he'd been over to see me this week.

"Isn't it amazing to think that the book could be strange to some people? I guess it's all just become so familiar to me. It's hard to think of someone reading it for the first time. All the new names. I guess it would seem pretty different."

I had to agree.

"She grew up without much religion, I think. I know she's a Catholic by name, and she said a few things about her confirmation and all that confession business, but I sure don't think she believes too much of anything. I probably wouldn't either, if I were her.

"I think her mother must be some kind of an alcoholic," I added quietly, after a pause.

Krestin shook his head.

"Sometimes I get pretty scared thinking about leaving for Brazil. There's a whole world out there that knows nothing about me, Katherine, and I know nothing about them, either. Why should they care what I have to say to them about Christ?"

"I sure don't know."

"Thanks for your vote of confidence!" There was a touch of anger in Krestin's voice that startled me.

"I didn't mean anything by it," I said quickly. "I think you're just a little uneasy about leaving."

"Just where are you lately, anyway, Katherine?"

Why is everyone asking me these questions, I thought. First Auntie. Now Krestin.

"I don't know, Krestin. I'm closer to where you are than I am to where Jilligan is. That much I know. But I still feel a little funny about some things."

"Well, why don't you do something about it!"

There was that odd sound of anger in Krestin's voice again.

"Why do you have to keep sitting in the middle? And why don't you ever talk to me about it all? Why do you keep listening to that Jilligan friend of yours? Don't you know that a testimony is the best thing you could ever have? Or has she messed your mind up about that, too?"

Krestin continued, though now his voice had softened.

"You sure don't talk much to me about her, but I'm not stupid, Kathy. I know strange things are cooking in that head of yours. Why do you let yourself think that way? Why can't you just take hold and press toward the mark?"

I wished I had the answers for Krestin. I wanted to tell him the things he wanted most to hear.

And that night, long after he had left, I was still awake, tossing in my bed, thinking of so many things.

Then, hardly aware of what I was doing, I found that I was praying. Praying hard and earnestly, not about passing a test or sleeping well or all the other stupid and insignificant things that I had habitually been praying for lately, but for things of the greatest eternal consequence, for things I really wanted to know.

Why had I never thought to pray like this before?

Oh, Father in Heaven, please *help me find my answers. Please cause me to be touched by thy Spirit. Please, Father in Heaven, if thou art up there, please hear me. I want to know.*

I talked for a long time in my mind, not in a particularly formal or well-spoken way, not even on my knees, but for me, at least, I prayed in a very real way. And I felt, quite certainly, that my prayers were being heard.

It seemed a wonderful thing to pray, something I had forgotten about for the past several months, a pouring forth of my thoughts and feelings.

Help me to know, I pleaded, as I drifted into sleep.

11

Why is it, I wonder still, that the seeds of faith must fall on different ground?

"I read your section 89 to my mother last night."

Jilligan and I were sitting in seminary, waiting for Brother Turner to show up. For some reason he was late.

"Do you know what she said to me? She said, 'I wish I had heard that twenty years ago. It's such good advice.' Can you believe that? My mother!

"My mother is such an embarrassment to me," Jilligan continued, after a pause, "with her drinking and her pills and her psychiatrists. You just don't know what it's like to have a mother like that. Your mother is home baking cookies and doing normal mother things, and when you need to talk to her, she's there. But mine isn't. Or if she's there, she's glazed over."

It was true. My mother was always there for us, although sometimes she probably wished she weren't. I knew I had a good family, even when I compared it to other families in my ward and stake. But when I looked even farther, to the unknown world beyond my own little boundaries, I began to see what a huge blessing it was to have a good home.

I was naive, I realized again, as I studied those honey brown waves of hair in front of me. But I realized, too, that I didn't want to know any more about what was out there just yet. I wanted to know all the good—all the beautiful literature and music and art and science—but I was not sure I wanted to know any details about the bad. And why did Jilligan go home and get drunk at Christmastime if her mother's drinking bothered her so much? It didn't make sense.

It was funny how things were beginning to form in my head all of a sudden. I had spent enough time wallowing in indecision and confusion, I realized. I had spent enough time thinking of all the bad things about faith—about some of its limitations. My experience with prayer the night before was real to me now. It had convinced me that I needed to start reaching outward instead of inward.

"Whatever are we waiting around here for, anyway? This man isn't going to show up. In Boston, we'd all just leave instead of hanging around here forever."

The door opened just then, and Brother Turner walked in, a bit dishevelled.

"So sorry I'm late. Thanks for waiting. My little boy fell down the stairs this morning and broke his arm. He's only three, but he actually broke it. He was howling and screaming." Brother Turner was unpacking his bookbag as he spoke to us. "And then I administered to him, and he calmed down in the very instant I spoke the words, as if the pain had somehow left him, or maybe he was suddenly able to deal with his feelings.

"Whatever—it made me realize how much I take for granted. Here I am, a high school seminary teacher, trying to instruct you in the great principles of our faith. Especially our history this year. Day after day, morning after morning, afternoon after afternoon. Sometimes I admit I start to lose my fire. But, my young friends, we are involved in such an enormous work here. It goes beyond what we can rationally understand. I saw that again this morning.

"Sure, there are faults. There are always faults to be found in the people who attempt to move the religion forward. For goodness' sake, Jesus' own Twelve certainly

120

had some problems, and they were with Him. But I bear my most solemn testimony to you all that the doctrines and principles our church teaches are those that will bring us eternal life. I have no doubt of it.

"Life isn't just some meaningless existence, some hodgepodge of feelings where we largely seek our own gain. It is a part of a vast eternal movement that began before we were born, and will continue on into the unknown regions of eternity."

Brother Turner paused. The room was very quiet. I felt as if I was in a testimony meeting.

"I can't understand it all. And yet the Spirit has borne witness to me that this is true.

"Well—enough preaching." He smiled at himself. "Let's get on to section 88. I think we have just about enough time to briefly cover it, although it probably could stand a lifetime of thought. This is the section where the Lord sends the Comforter to be with them — the Holy Spirit, the promise of eternal life, and the glory of the celestial kingdom. And He talks about the Light of Christ.

"Let's see." Brother Turner looked over the class. "Jilligan!" He smiled as he called her name. "Can I get you to read 11 through 13 there, in 88?"

Jilligan turned her page, then began to read. Her clear, high, careful pronunciation filled the room, her accent more subtle for the moment.

" 'And the light which shineth, which giveth you light, is through him who enlighteneth your eyes, which is the same light that quickeneth your understandings; which light proceedeth forth from the presence of God to fill the immensity of space—the light which is in all things, which giveth life to all things, which is the law by which all things are governed, even the power of God who sitteth upon his throne, who is in the bosom of eternity, who is in the midst of all things.' "

Jilligan's voice had become progressively slower and more quiet as she read.

"Thanks, Jilligan. There it is then. The power of the light of the Holy Spirit, that rolls through all things, that

121

has existed in an eternal round. It is this light that gives life to all things, that quickens your understandings, and enlightens your mind. It is this power that witnesses to the truth of the gospel, that fills us with its light. And when we do receive that great sense of the truth of what we believe, it does fill us with a feeling of light."

Jilligan raised her hand.

"Where do those feelings come from? Are they in our brain? Are they in our mind? How come some people feel them and others don't? Like when I read that scripture just now, I felt a . . ." Jilligan paused. "a feeling, I guess. But where does that come from?" She paused a moment; then, making her eyes round, she said, "Maybe it's catching."

Several of us laughed.

Ignoring her dramatics, Brother Turner replied, "I guess I'd have to say that those feelings come partly into your mind, but they also come from somewhere else. I'd say it's more in the heart. You might call it the soul. It's the place where the Holy Spirit can speak to us."

"Are we all born that way?"

"I think so, although some of us choose to ignore it, or have never been taught to recognize those feelings for what they are."

It was time to go.

"Jilligan," I said, as we gathered our things. "You were great in there."

"What do you mean?"

"The questions you asked. The things Brother Turner said. It was good."

Jilligan made no response. She just looked at me, shrugging her shoulders.

"I guess," was all she said. "If you can believe it."

It was almost time to say good-bye to Auntie, to end all that had been so good and warm between us. I felt as if she had died already, the parting seemed so final.

Auntie's house was completely empty. There was even a homemade For Sale sign on the lawn now. Auntie had given power of attorney to my father should anyone want to buy her home.

I hated the sight of that sign. It seemed somehow as if a whole lifetime was for sale. And part of that life was mine.

Auntie wanted me to go through her house one more time with her to make sure she hadn't forgotten anything.

"Be my eyes one last time, Kathy."

But I could find nothing in her home, only the large empty spaces that once had been full of Auntie Anna.

Outside her kitchen window, her rich green lawn was covered with snow, frozen under the whiteness, her flowers dormant.

"It's easier to leave in the winter," Auntie had said to my father. "If I had to feel as if I were leaving my garden —all my growing things—I think I would not be able to do it. But to leave a sleeping, unfragrant garden . . ."

"What will we do without your bouquet every Sunday?" my father said quietly, half to himself.

"Marcie says I can take care of her flower beds. Did I tell you that?"

Auntie ate dinner with us that evening. She would sleep on our sofa bed for the night. My mother had insisted. Then my father would take her to the airport in the morning.

Several people stopped by to see her after dinner, bidding her additional farewells and a safe trip. Even some of her old students came.

"How did you ever know?" Auntie asked.

It was hard and happy for everyone, for we all knew Auntie would not be back, and yet we knew she must go.

After all the people left, it was my turn to say goodbye. In all likelihood there would be no time in the morning. Auntie's plane was leaving at seven, and I knew I did not want to go to the airport. I wanted to do my crying at home.

"Ah, my little Katherine," Auntie said. "I do feel the great finality of this good-bye. Unless you manage to get to California before I die . . ." There was no need to finish.

"Things will be good for you at Marcie's," I said. "You do need to go back there."

Auntie sat silently at my desk chair, in front of the picture of Christ and the trumpets. I sat on my bed. I thought of all the years I had known her. There was so much kindness and goodness in my life because of her, so much conversation.

We said our good-byes quietly.

"Be true," Auntie simply said. "I will see you again."

Those were the last words she spoke to me.

Be true.

As I lay in bed that night, my tears spent, I knew that Auntie's leaving would change me. I felt somehow that now I would face myself. I would stretch forward with maturity and nurture my faith, or acknowledge that I would never know what was true and right in life.

Auntie would want me to do that, to reach out in the strength of my own heart and find my answers. I would move forward. I would seize my life and seek for a deep and abiding testimony. It was my right as a child of God.

I would be true.

Krestin had wanted to go out with Jilligan ever since his conversation with her before Christmas. I had told him I certainly didn't mind if he did. And after he heard about her comments in seminary on Monday, he said he knew he had to do it.

They went to Sundance together on Saturday. Jilligan had never skied before, and Krestin wasn't exactly a whiz at it, although he did go occasionally with friends.

The next day as I sat beside him in sacrament meeting, his arm draped behind me on the pew without touching me, I could hardly wait to hear how it had gone for them the day before.

"I'll tell you when we get home," was all he had said to my eager inquiry. He had not even smiled or frowned. There was no indication as to how it all had gone.

"It was really an experience," Krestin told me now, as we started our walk home from church. "I can almost see why you could start to get your head spun around a little bit with her. She's so pretty and all, and so well-spoken, and athletic. She skis practically as good as me after one day there! And she has that earnestness about her that is irresistible. But then you're always kind of wondering if she's half pulling your leg, after all.

"She told me a lot more about her mom—things I don't even want to tell you, Kathy—and I guess that's been a pretty weird kind of influence to grow up under. It sure made me feel like the simple-minded little kid from Utah, listening to all she's experienced in life already. Not that things like that don't happen out here, but they sure haven't happened to me!"

We turned the corner down 543 East.

"The world is so huge, isn't it, Kathy? I realized it yesterday as I never realized it before. You know, I used to sit there and watch the news reports from Vietnam and see all those bloody and dead men, and those Vietnamese running around in the jungles, and I used to think, How does this all fit together? Can God really love us all?

"I felt like that yesterday again. Like it's all so immense. And the world really isn't all that good. I mean, it is and it isn't. Do you know what I mean?"

I nodded.

"And then I remembered God's tears in Moses 7. He was so sad because of the wickedness of the people. Man left to his own agency is a mess. Of course He would cry."

The mountaintops were pure white with snow, I noticed, a backdrop of pristine whiteness above our little homes.

"So here we are, Katherine, this small bunch of people, proclaiming to hold on to His truth in the face of all the madness and unkindness in the world.

"And you know what? I really think we have it. I really think Heavenly Father is so happy to have this group of people to serve Him in the face of all this madness. I so want to help people to see that.

"Your friend Jilligan, there, I don't think she'll ever see it. She flat out told me that she'd probably throw the Book of Mormon in the garbage when she's done here, because she doesn't want it to haunt her for the rest of her life. I think she's really had some moments when she's probably felt the Spirit touch her. But you know, if she doesn't listen to the things she feels, she'll just go on laughing at it all.

"Faith is so real to me, Katherine." Krestin's voice was full of excitement. "It's as real as you and me walking home from church together. I can't help it. I feel it so strong sometimes."

Krestin put his arm on my shoulder and pulled me to him, an expression of his exuberant faith needing to be shared more than anything else, I thought.

"I sure hope I'm a good missionary," he said.

And then he laughed to himself—a private, mysterious, joyous little sound.

12

I never did see Auntie again, although she lived several years longer after she moved back with Marcie. She lived long enough to see her oldest grandchild leave on a mission. And to see Marcie slowly begin to attend church again.

We wrote often in the beginning; Marcie even called a few times. But once I got busy at BYU our correspondence settled down to a Christmas exchange, although I remained always aware, somehow, of her existence on the earth.

I received word of Auntie's death while I was spending a semester in Israel. I had finally realized my dream to see the Holy Land. BYU had a program there, and I worked and saved all that I could to get myself there, to walk where the Savior had walked.

It was the right place to be to hear of Auntie's death. I spent an afternoon in Gethsemane after I heard, mourning the loss of Auntie's presence here, yet knowing completely that the bonds of death had been broken, and that I would see her again.

And she would see me.

Jilligan and I sat in the same room, our number two pencils in hand. Every now and then I couldn't keep myself from glancing in her direction. Occasionally I felt her look my way, although I made sure my eyes never met hers.

We were taking the SATs together. I had no need of them. I had already taken the ACTs, but Jilligan had forcefully persuaded me not to close all options on where I would go to school.

"Most of the Eastern schools don't use the ACTs. You've just got to take these in case you suddenly change your mind and want to go to a different school."

And so I'd talked to my parents about it, and they had agreed it would be kind of fun to see how I did on them. They wrote the check and I mailed in the application.

"Maybe you'll beat that old Jilligan out on this test," my mother said with startling glee, as she shovelled some oatmeal into my bowl this morning.

"I don't know, Mom. That's not the reason I'm taking the test."

But as I sat there in the exam room, my pencil shading in the oval for the question at hand, I realized how fiercely I wanted to beat Jilligan on this test. I felt every bit of my brain fired with the desire to do better than she did.

"How'd you think it went?" Jilligan asked me, meeting me at my desk as soon as all the papers had been turned in. "Kind of fun, wasn't it?"

I shrugged.

"I guess time will tell," she said.

It would be April by the time we would hear.

Auntie Anna's departure was not the only great wrenching my heart would feel that winter. Like a strangely twisted play, all of the major actors in my life were suddenly making their exits.

"Well, Sister Gardner, I'm off to the LTM tomorrow."

"I'll surely miss you, Krestin. You brightened up my life."

"I'll treasure that assessment of my personality for the next two years, Sister Gardner. I'm sure there'll be at least a few companions who will entirely disagree with you. But that's part of what a mission is for, isn't it? To drive yourself and your companion crazy?"

I could tell Krestin was nervous. His jokes were worse than usual.

My father shook Krestin's hand, then threw his other arm around him in a hug. "You'll be a good one, Krestin. Just be sensitive. And go easy on yourself."

"I'll remember that, Brother Gardner. Go easy and be sensitive."

Mom and Dad conveniently exited to the family room, and Krestin and I were left to ourselves in the living room. The boys were already in bed.

"Now that we've come this far, there really isn't very much to say, is there?" Krestin said. He had on his grungiest jeans, wearing them for the last time before he traded them in for a steady diet of suits and ties.

"Can I tell you that I'm suddenly scared to death? I mean, how on earth am I ever going to learn enough Portuguese and then teach people the gospel in it? It's a big enough job in English, isn't it? I am so filled with the feeling of 'Why on earth am I doing this?' "

"You're doing this because you're a good man, maybe one of the best around." My response came easily.

Krestin shook his head and rolled his eyes.

"Besides," I said, wanting him to know how good and true I thought he was, "I think you have a gift for speaking the simple truth with love."

"Well, thank you, Katherine. Thanks so much. That's probably the nicest thing you could have said to me. I'm going to write it on my brain and try to live up to it. Speaking the truth with love. I hope so, Kathy, I really do."

I didn't know what more to say. I didn't want my eyes to meet his, but they did, and we both laughed. Krestin reached for my hand.

"I went to the temple last night with my mom and dad one last time. They wanted to go with me tonight, but I said, no, I had to come say good-bye to you on my last night. I hope you don't mind.

129

"It's all so enormous, Katherine. This really is a great eternal plan we're involved in. Our baptism and our little callings are such a small part of what's out there. We're talking about becoming more Christ-like in every way we can. We're talking about really trying for perfection. It hit me so hard last night during the endowment session. This is just so vast, this gospel. And I'm so little."

Krestin left soon after. I wished desperately that I had gotten a gift for him, something to give him in return for all those years we'd been together. He was such a good, good friend.

"So we'll write, right?"

"Of course."

"And maybe we'll get together again at the other end of this thing. I do think I love you, Katherine. I do feel that we're meant to be together."

He kissed me.

"God bless," he said. And he was gone.

I heard the sound of his engine start up, then heard the distant sound of his shifting as he drove down the quiet Orem streets, further and further from my home and from all that we had been.

He would speak the truth with love, I knew.

He always did.

13

I wonder if we all have a moment where we mark the beginning of our testimony. I suppose most converts have one—a space in time when the Spirit fills them and bears witness to the truth.

I know my husband does. He often tells people how he was sitting on the grass outside the law school, reading the Book of Mormon in between classes, when he felt a great and warming sensation come upon him and fill his body. He had been praying and fasting since he had first started the discussions—something he could actually perceive with his senses. And then that happened, unplanned and unexpected.

Not only did he feel the warmth, but deep inside him, he felt the joy. Joy as he had never known, he told me on the phone that evening. He had experienced that mighty change of heart, and had felt to sing the song of redeeming love. He was baptized shortly after.

I have my moment too, my beginning point, my own deep witness that Christ lives, that Joseph Smith was a prophet, and that living prophets direct us today.

My family had two traditions, both centered around the same place. We went to Temple Square every year at

Christmastime, and we went there again just before or after April conference. We went in December to see the lights; we went in April to see the flowers. And we went both times just to be there—to feel a closeness to the center of the Church. I loved to go.

I felt a sense of history when I was there. Here walked the early apostles of the Church. Here was the place Joseph Smith had longed to find for his people, the Zion removed and safe from the threat of the mobs, a place apart.

My little brothers loved to go to watch the movies that the visitors' center always had available. Robert and Suzanne and I used to do the same. I thought of them as I stood there now.

My father was already cornering an older missionary couple, asking them if Jim and Bill could watch a few movies while they were here.

"And take the tour, too!" Jim added, pulling at my father's sleeve. "Couldn't we do that, too?"

I had already told Dad I wanted to wander around by myself this afternoon. I didn't want to have to take care of my little brothers this time. I wanted just to think. Mom and Dad assured me they would shepherd them.

I went outside, wanting to be back in the beautiful spring air. Just last Sunday thousands of people had filled Temple Square, listening to the voice of the prophets. And I had watched much of it at home, wishing to go there for conference sometime soon.

Tulips filled the beds outside the visitors' center. I walked the pattern we had walked for years at Christmastime—down between the Tabernacle and the Assembly Hall, over to the statue of the handcart pioneers, to the quiet side of the temple (as Robert had always called it), and then back to the visitors' center entrance.

In my mind I went over the events of the past year. Could it be possible that last spring Jilligan hadn't even been here? And didn't we come with Krestin last spring? And with Robert? And Suzanne had just married Mike. And I hadn't even learned how to give Auntie her shots.

And now here I was, almost seventeen years old. It didn't seem possible. How could all that time have passed, with all those thoughts and feelings!

I went inside. My little brothers were huddled around a screen. My father stood nearby, thumbing through a book. He winked at me.

I saw my mom over by the Harry Anderson murals, marvelling at his gift, I knew. I walked over to be with her.

"I just love to look at these pictures whenever I come," she told me, as she had told me on other trips here, shaking her head slightly from side to side. "What a gift! Everything seems so real to me when I look at these pictures."

The last picture in the series was of Christ commissioning the Twelve.

I thought of Krestin. He had written me only once since he had entered the LTM a month ago. It had been a little bit of an adjustment, but learning a language was coming more easily than it had in high school. "There really is a spirit here," he had written.

"I'm just going to stay here for a little while," Mom said, interrupting my thoughts.

I wandered up the gently sloping circular walkway, past the murals of the moon and the stars. I thought about time and about space, about our mind and our soul. I thought of Krestin and Auntie Anna, of Jilligan and Marcie, of my mother and father. I thought of the various ways we all accepted and rejected and believed and loved the Lord.

I thought of the vast regions of the earth, of all the people I would never know who had heard and who had not heard of the Savior and His church, who believed and who did not believe. What lay ahead for us all? I wondered.

I heard Jilligan's voice asking me where it all came from. Where did we get our capacity to feel spiritual things? Was it inherited? Was it a product of our environment?

I stood before the Christus statue.

And something filled me then. I felt it rise and swell and expand my mind and my soul. For an instant, I felt completely and surely the truth of my faith. I felt it in some deepest part of me, beyond where my words and thought and empirical knowlege could go.

I knew the Savior lived, and that He had bound me to Him — and that He would bind all mankind to Him if He could. And I knew this was His church.

The feelings came from within and without — a part of my mind and a part of my heart. They were real. They made me want to run and laugh and sing and share and finally, simply cry.

Although the world was huge and filled with problems and trials and knowledge beyond my understanding, still, I knew in that priceless moment how deeply we all were in need of the universal atonement of Christ.

I knew it.

14

My memory fails me suddenly. Perhaps it is because Johnny is banging on the piano downstairs, and Mark is madly screaming for a chance to share in the fun too.

I will close my door to it all for this hour, I decide. There's a chance they will not kill each other. Perhaps Annie can keep her little brothers calm.

I do remember the horrible fear I felt after I'd gotten my SAT scores in the mail. Jilligan received hers the same day and called me that afternoon to hear how I'd done. I made her tell me her marks first. I scored forty points higher than she did.

"I told you you should have taken the PSAT," she said.

"What would it have mattered," I said.

And I meant it.

And I did become editor of the school paper, although Jilligan insisted on running against me even in that.

And then June came and she, too, was gone.

"Hello, Katherine."

The young woman who stood grinning before me in the doorway was unfamiliar. I felt my brow knot up in confusion.

135

"Oh, come on, Katherine, don't—"

"Jilligan?" I interrupted. "Jilligan!"

Her smile told me it was true. But where was all her beautiful long hair?

"You cut your hair."

"Is that all you're going to say? Can't I at least have a hug?"

Had I ever hugged her before? I thought, as I put my arms around her slender shoulders now. She smelled sweet.

"Isn't it great to see each other again after all this time! How long has it been now? More than a year?"

I could barely respond.

"When did you cut your hair?" I asked. "You look so completely different. And those glasses . . ."

Jilligan's hair was cut in a pageboy. It was perfectly straight and turned under and she had bangs now. It looked as though it had been bleached. And she wore sunglasses with dark frames and pale purple lenses. It was amazing I had known it was her at all.

"Why did you cut . . ."

"Oh, good grief! Is that all you're going to talk about? My hair?"

She was laughing at me still, I thought, even after all this time.

"I cut my hair when I graduated from high school. I did it because I wanted to look older. I do look older, don't I?"

I was still trying to absorb the shock of seeing her again.

"Can't I come in?"

"Of course," I said dumbly. "My parents are gone with my brothers today. They had a pinewood derby. I'm watching my sister's little girl. She was born that year you lived here, remember?" I felt like my speech was coming out so slowly.

"I guess I do," Jilligan said, "but it seems kind of foggy now. I never even met your sister. Can I sit down, Katherine?"

"Sure. Let's sit in the living room. It's easier to hear Jennifer then, if she cries."

"So you're a devoted aunt, then?"

"Yes." I loved my little niece passionately. She was a perfect thing—chubby, with great gray eyes and strawberry blonde curly hair.

"She's just two years now."

"And Krestin? Is he home yet?" Jilligan asked.

"He just got back last month. He had a wonderful mission."

"You two still hitting it off?" She shook her head in a funny way as she asked me.

It was so good to see him again, was all I said.

It was hard to talk to Jilligan. We had written on and off over the past two years. She had even come out to see me once last year, briefly, when we were both still in high school. Her father had come back for two days to Salt Lake then, and she had "tagged along," as she had said. I had met her in Salt Lake.

But this visit was such a surprise. And something had changed.

Gradually, after the first fifteen minutes or so, our conversation became easier. And yet, I felt a need to protect myself from this girl, too. It was an unfamiliar feeling. I felt her a stranger—almost as if it was the first week of my junior year all over again.

She was talking about college now. She had managed to get into some pre-med courses, even as a freshman.

"I had taken so many AP courses last year that they let me get on into some more advanced stuff."

She wasn't going to Harvard after all. She had written me about that change in her plans months ago. She was going somewhere in Boston, though. It was a new program, she said, one that allowed her to finish college and med school in a shorter amount of time. It was connected with a hospital there in Boston, where she would be required to do her internship. She was in the pilot class, and she was the only woman. I got the idea that it was quite an achievement to be in the program.

"And it's so stressful. I feel all this pressure on me to be the best. Luckily Charlie and I have moved in together. I don't think I could make it without him."

"You and Charlie are living together?" My mind was still a few steps behind.

"Living and sleeping and eating together. You know. Does that shock you, Katherine?"

Why did she keep calling me *Katherine?* I stood and went to look out the living room window. I felt claustrophobic. The thought of her sleeping with someone filled me with disgust.

Why did she come here, anyway?

"Listen, Katherine," Jilligan went on. "You've really got to think about this religion of yours. It's like living in a steel trap all your life. I've talked about you to so many people out there, and they're all convinced you've been brainwashed into believing the stuff you believe.

"You've got to get out of here for a while and test your wings."

She paused for a moment. I half expected her to pull out a cigarette and light it. But she didn't. She was just catching her breath.

"God doesn't talk to us. Well, maybe He talks to the Pope, or somebody important like that, but He sure doesn't talk to you and me. People will think you're crazy if they think you've had some religious experience. There's no room for it in life. Why don't you get out of BYU and come on out to Boston?"

I let Jilligan talk.

I stood at the window and looked across the street. The family who had bought Auntie's house came out as I stood there—a father, a mother, and five little children. They loved to garden. They had kept Auntie's roses as beautifully as she had ever done them. Their kids screamed a lot when they played, but they were such a good family. Little Robbie saw me at the window and waved. They all packed into their beat-up Suburban and drove off.

Jilligan was still talking.

"We already cut open our first cadaver," she was saying. "It's as gruesome as you can imagine. I mean, here's this body, and then you stick your knife into it. But after the first hour, you forget it ever was any sort of a person. Might as well be a frog. I think ours was just some drunk they found dead in the gutter, anyway.

"After you get used to it, though, it's like a giant treasure hunt. The surgeon keeps poking around for different parts—pulling them out like he's found some great treasure for us to share in. It's really kind of fun. 'Here's the heart. Here's the kidney. Here's the liver.'

"One guy started to feel pretty sick, so they took him out."

I thought of Krestin's homecoming talk as Jilligan went on. Krestin had just spoken in our ward the previous Sunday. He had spent two years among the warmest and simplest people he had ever known, people who could grasp faith in an instant, he said.

They were the most wonderful years of his life, he had said. A precious gift. It was a complete honor to bring the restored gospel to those beautiful people.

He seemed so different to me now. He seemed a true saint—so purged of the world and of all worldly thoughts. I could tell how totally he had immersed himself in the things of the Spirit. He had been a great missionary. And he was having a hard time getting used to being just a regular person, he told me.

I really hadn't seen too much of him in the three weeks since he'd gotten back.

"Then they let us do some brain explorations."

Jilligan was still talking. She paused for a minute.

"Do you have anything to drink?" she asked, laughing. "I feel like a real motor-mouth here, but I've got to get back to Salt Lake at four. What time is it now? Two-thirty? Well, another half hour and then I've got to go."

I got her a glass of lemonade.

"Nothing stronger?" she teased. "Katherine. Anyway," she said before swallowing a great gulp of lemonade, "I've come to tell you that there's nothing there. There's nothing there that seems to me the least bit spiritual in the whole human body. We're machines. Even our mind is a machine. There's nothing labeled *soul.*

"There's electricity and blood and chemicals and flesh. And water.

"And there's just no room for your spirit stuff. People think the way they do because of their environment and because they're chemically put together the way they are. And sometimes the machine breaks down, and a part has to be repaired, or replaced, and sometimes you can't fix it. And that's all there is to it.

"Don't get me wrong. I'll love my patients and I'll be compassionate and caring towards them, but I'm just telling you that I reject the ideas that you Mormons teach."

I had been standing for the longest time, standing and looking down at Jilligan as she spoke.

Who was this person? I thought.

Had we really been together in high school?

This was a different person from the one I had known. I did not want to sit down next to her. I felt better standing, listening to her from a distance.

My niece let out a cry.

"There's Jenny," I said, thankful to be summoned. I left the living room without a word. I had set the playpen up in my bedroom.

Jenny was awake, all soft and pink-cheeked. The pattern on the blanket had left a little crease in her face. She saw me and lifted her arms above her head, laughing merrily. We had become good friends during the week of my sister's visit.

"Jenny!" I said, the magical tone we used with babies filling my voice. "Jenny! Is it time to get up, little girl?"

I lifted her out of the playpen. She wrapped her arms around me, babbling happily in my ear, then grabbing my nose with her hand. I stood there in my room, holding on to this warm little soul, thinking of the girl in the living room. I thought of the great love that had brought my niece to this earth.

I believe it, I thought simply, as I felt her warm breath on my face. I believe it all. I know we are children of our Heavenly Father. I don't have all the answers, and I expect I never will. Faith is so complex, requiring humility and sensitivity. But oh! I feel it to be true.

That we are complicated people, I knew. That I had

difficulties now and then, I knew. But oh! there was that silent, steady witness in my heart, the feeling that said, Doubt not! Fear not! press on toward the mark. Hold fast to that which is good.

The picture of Christ and the angels filled my vision. What could I do but press on. I had received a witness, and I could not deny it.

I carried Jenny out to the living room.

"Oh, she's beautiful!" Jilligan said.

Jenny was usually shy with strangers, but when I put her down she walked right over to Jilligan, curious to find this new person in the house. Jilligan had put her sunglasses down on the couch, and Jenny wanted them.

Jilligan gave them to her to play with.

"Aren't those strange things?" she said. "You like to touch them, don't you?"

Jennifer held them gently, then began to bang them.

"Oh, look at the time!" Jilligan said, glancing at her watch. "I've got to get out of here. Dad's got some people he wants me to meet for dinner, and then we're flying out tomorrow morning."

She took the glasses from Jenny.

"Katherine," she said, "I hate to run. Kind of like a whirlwind visit, isn't it? Forty-five minutes of chat. Please write me. Call me. Do something! Let's keep in touch. And if you decide to come to Boston, please come see me."

She moved to the front door, opening it.

I felt a sudden panic fill me then. She couldn't leave! Not yet! I had not had a chance to respond. She couldn't leave me like that! It wouldn't be fair.

"Jilligan!" I said. "Jilligan!" I felt as though I was calling an inattentive child.

She looked at me then, waiting expectantly.

"Jilligan, I just have to tell you." I was stumbling inside.

How can I ever express myself now, I thought.

"I know it's true," I blurted out. "I know you think there's no such thing as the Spirit, but Jilligan, I've felt it fill me."

I told her about that day in Salt Lake, about how the

141

warm, real feeling had spread through me, filling me with joy and certainty. I told her it had come from another source — not from my mind, not from my own wishes — but that it had come, filling me, declaring without a doubt that Christ lived and that He loved us. I told her about the many experiences since then — the joy that would fill me as I studied the scriptures, or as I heard the prophet speak.

I told her that I had come to the conclusion that she probably had been right — that maybe I was a smart person, that I probably was a little more intellectual than those around me, and that I knew I thought about things more deeply than others. And that maybe I would see the conflicts in life and in faith more than others.

But I knew that the glory of God was intelligence. That intelligence was not our own glory, but His. I had read the wonderful words of the prophets, of Brigham Young, counselling us to learn all that we could. I knew, too, I said, that there was a danger in thinking that we could ever know it all on our own. Life was so empty and meaningless without faith, I said.

"And Jilligan," I said, "I have these moments, these indescribable moments, when I am walking on the BYU campus late at night, coming home from the library, when I feel swelling up inside of me a great sense of the love of God for all His children, regardless of their religion. I feel it fill me and permeate every particle of my body.

"I just know God lives. There is no doubt in my mind or in my heart. And we are all poor sinners in one way or another, desperately in need of Christ's atonement. And the Church helps us to move in a more Christlike direction. I know that.

"And Jilligan," I said, and my voice was shaking now, trembling with emotion and with the energy required for me to speak my thoughts to Jilligan, "Jilligan, I love you."

My voice cracked. I had never said or thought those words before, but in the moment of my speaking them, I knew them to be true.

"And I know God loves you, too. I don't know why you feel you haven't gotten any answers, but please know this, Jilligan. I know it. Please remember that."

There was silence then—heavy, effulgent stillness. I was trembling within and without.

Jilligan looked at me for a moment. Her eyes quickly avoided mine. She fixed her gaze on my niece's movements in the living room.

"What more can we say, then?" was all she said.

I stood in the front doorway and watched her walk down the path to the sidewalk. I watched her as she got into her car. The window rolled smoothly down.

"Your niece is beautiful!" she called to me. And she waved a hand out her window. She put her sunglasses on.

"Fingerprints!" she called.

And then she was gone.

Jenny had walked over to me. She pulled on my pantleg, requesting my attention. I reached down and picked her up, holding her closely to me.

"Jenny," I said softly.

And then I began to cry—great, hard gulps of tears, filling me with shudders of pain and of joy and of certainty and of sorrow, wrenching the last of my childhood from me, pulling me gently, urgently, in the only direction my maturing faith could travel.

My path, although not easy, was perfectly clear.

15

We are holding family home evening. Annie is eight. She will be baptized tomorrow.

My husband stands in the living room with her. He bends slightly so Annie can grasp onto his arm. He is telling her what will happen tomorrow, how he will hold her and lift her backwards into the water, just as the Savior taught.

He is saying that he was not baptized until he was twenty-five. He is telling her how special she is to have the blessing of faith so young.

His voice breaks.

"Daddy!" Annie says, looking up with large eyes. "Why are you crying?"

"Because sometimes the Spirit is so strong, Annie, and I know that it's true."

I wipe the tears from my own eyes. John and Mark climb onto my lap.